"Did you want

"Yeah." Kirk reached ... door. "You."

Before Tonya could speak, he caught her in his arms and kissed her. His kiss tasted of urgency, of desperation. He pressed her tightly against his body while his hands roamed over her, reawakening every nerve ending. His hands molded her breasts, traveled along her thighs, set her on fire. She struggled with his buttons, dragged his shirt apart to expose his chest and kissed him with the same wild desperation.

"I want you. Now," he said raggedly.

He lifted her, fitting her closer to him, and set her against the desk. She heard a thud as her dictionary slid off and landed on the floor. Her hand fell to the side, and pens and paper clips flew in all directions. Tonya squirmed as a fevered excitement tore through her. Then suddenly Kirk was over her, pressing her down against the cool wood of the desk. Papers scattered, her in-box crashed to the floor.

Startled by the noise, Tonya glanced first at the floor and then at Kirk. She grinned. "Hello, did you have an appointment?"

The moment sassy Tonya Brewster roared down her cousin Samantha's driveway in her red Jaguar in *The Great Chili Caper,* author **Lorna Michaels** knew that Tonya needed a book of her own. "There's definitely something appealing about a heroine who can't hold a job, get a date or drive within the speed limit," Lorna says with a laugh. "Maybe it's because so many of us can identify with her." Lorna lives near Houston, Texas, with her family.

Books by Lorna Michaels

HARLEQUIN TEMPTATION
523—THE RELUCTANT HUNK
584—THE GREAT CHILI CAPER

HARLEQUIN SUPERROMANCE
412—BLESSING IN DISGUISE
503—A MATTER OF PRIVILEGE
528—SEASON OF LIGHT
633—THE RELUCTANT BODYGUARD

THE TROUBLE WITH TONYA
Lorna Michaels

Harlequin Books

TORONTO • NEW YORK • LONDON
AMSTERDAM • PARIS • SYDNEY • HAMBURG
STOCKHOLM • ATHENS • TOKYO • MILAN
MADRID • WARSAW • BUDAPEST • AUCKLAND

To Rita Gallagher,
With love and thanks for helping me begin.

ISBN 0-373-25732-5

THE TROUBLE WITH TONYA

1

"WE'VE GOT TO STOP MEETING like this." Tonya Brewster grinned at the red-haired, freckle-faced cop who was writing her a ticket.

"We could if you'd quit speeding." Officer Rusty O'Connor signed his name with a flourish and looked up, his blue eyes twinkling. "What's the excuse this time?"

Tonya sighed dramatically. "I'm late for a meeting."

He raised a brow. "Pretty lame. You know," he added, tapping his fingers on the door frame of the lipstick red Jaguar, "I'd hate to see you smash up this baby."

Tonya stuffed the ticket into the recesses of her leather bag, then ran her hands lovingly over the steering wheel. "Never."

"Then *slow down*."

"Okay." As she pulled back into traffic, he waved and Tonya beeped her horn. She glanced at the dashboard clock. No way she'd make the board meeting on time now.

She wondered why her grandfather had appointed her to complete her mother's term on the board of the Brewster Charitable Foundation when her parents left to set up a branch of the family food business in Moscow. Clint Brewster rarely did anything without a reason, but when she'd asked him why he'd picked her out of all the available family members, he'd simply said, "Because you can do it." She did have more free time than most of the others. She guessed that was reason enough.

Tonya shrugged. As long as she was late anyway, she might as well enjoy the ride. She rolled her window down halfway to take advantage of the springlike February day, turned the radio to one of Houston's soft rock stations and sang along.

Twenty minutes later, windblown from the ride and out of breath from dashing across the parking lot, she tiptoed into the conference room and slid into a chair next to her cousin Samantha.

Sam gave her a sharp kick under the table. "You're late," she whispered.

"Tell me about it." Even if her encounter with the law hadn't slowed her down, she still wouldn't have been on time. As she'd left her town house and gotten into her car, she'd noticed a stray kitten in the driveway. Poor thing had been mewling like a little lost soul. Immediately identifying with the kitten, she'd just had to pick him up, take him into her town house and give him something to eat. After he lapped up a saucer of milk, Tonya had spread an old towel on the utility room floor and left the kitten curled up and purring contentedly. But then she'd had to rush.

She glanced at her grandfather and received a stern look in return. Unrepentant, Tonya turned toward August Parker, who was reading the minutes of the last board meeting in the deep, resonant tones he used in the courtroom.

She stole a glance at Sam. Her cousin looked, as always, like a Dresden figurine. She sat with eyes fixed on Mr. Parker and hands folded on the table in front of her. Tonya tapped her foot. How did Sam manage to look so interested, so composed? Surely she had other things on her mind. Like sex. Her marriage to private detective Wade Phillips had barely passed the honeymoon stage.

When the board broke for lunch, Tonya started to get up to join the others milling around the room, but Sam put a hand on her shoulder. "What happened this morning? Did you run late with a customer?"

"Nope, a kitten." When Sam looked puzzled, Tonya continued. "I don't have customers anymore. I quit my job last week."

Sam looked surprised. "Why? I thought Desirée's Boutique was *the* place to work."

"Not for me. I got tired cooing over those silly society matrons. 'Oh, yes, Mrs. Jennings, this dress is *you*,' when the outfit made her look like Minnie Mouse. Then there were the simpering debutantes."

Her cousin's brows shot up. "You were a debutante yourself not so long ago."

"*I* never simpered," Tonya reminded Sam, tossing her head. She glanced at the door and smiled. "Ah, there's lunch, the best part of these board meetings, or is that bored-stiff meetings?"

"Hush," Sam whispered. "Here comes Granddad."

Clint Brewster came up behind them, placed a hand on each granddaughter's shoulder and gazed down at them with penetrating blue eyes. "Samantha, your grandmother says to bring that husband of yours and come for dinner Thursday. You, too, Tonya. What time do you finish at the dress shop?"

Tonya cleared her throat. "I don't. That is, I've finished for good at Desirée's. I'm...unemployed at the moment." Her grandfather's eyes narrowed. "But—"

Before she could finish, someone called to him and he strode away.

Tonya turned to Sam. "But I have something in mind. I talked to Betsy Potter, the owner of that new mystery bookstore, Whodunit. She needs help setting up some mystery weekends around the state. Murder, mystery and mayhem.

Just my style, huh? Besides—" she grinned slyly "—I have connections in the mystery book field."

Her cousin looked horrified. "You didn't tell her about Wade, did you?" Sam's husband, a bestselling mystery writer, wrote under a pen name and kept his real identity under wraps.

"Don't worry, cuz," Tonya said. "His secret is safe with me." She took a bite of the salad Niçoise that had been placed before her and eyed her grandfather across the room, wondering what he'd think about her new job prospect. Not much, probably. They'd had plenty of "discussions" about her work habits.

In a family of worker bees, Tonya was the lone butterfly. She couldn't help it, could she, that her attention span was short, that she flitted from one "career" to another? Something more enticing, more interesting always beckoned on the horizon.

Sometimes she envied her relatives with their clear-cut goals. They all knew where they were going. But what was the fun in that? She'd take the byway over the highway anytime. After college she'd worked in an herb shop, next at a singles resort, then spent a season on a cruise ship. She'd helped a friend publicize a heart-healthy catering service, and that had led to some fund-raising for the American Heart Association. Later, she'd helped set up a resale shop to benefit the Cystic Fibrosis Foundation, her family's pet charity. In between, she'd indulged her thirst for travel. The Whodunit job would be interesting and would satisfy her wanderlust, at least on a small scale.

When the board reconvened after lunch, Tonya considered where her first mystery trip might take place as she listened with half an ear to Janus Nichols, the foundation director, discuss an inner-city agency that had applied for funds.

Galveston. A rambling Victorian house with the ghost of a seafarer roaming the attic.

"The Our Kids Center is dedicated to setting youngsters on the right path before they lose their footing," Nichols said. "Their mission is to provide programs that keep youngsters off the streets, out of gangs, away from drugs."

Or El Paso. Smugglers crossing the Rio Grande.

Nichols droned on. The board voted to fund the agency, with one stipulation...

Maybe she'd plan a murder mystery aboard a cruise ship. The captain did it...

"Tonya?"

Her grandfather's voice intruded on a delightfully vivid fantasy unfolding on the promenade deck. "Hmm?"

Sam pinched her arm, eliciting a gasp.

"Tonya."

Rubbing her arm, she turned to her grandfather. "Yes, sir?"

"You can take this on—"

Tonya blinked. "Uh..."

"Since you're not presently employed," he continued.

Tonya lifted her hand to her mouth, pretending to cover a cough. "What's he talking about?" she hissed at Sam.

"Weren't you listening?"

"Not really." She gave her purse a nudge and toppled it from the table. "Uh, excuse me." She bent down to retrieve it and jerked on Sam's skirt. Her cousin joined her under the table. "Well?" Tonya prodded.

"We voted to fund the Our Kids Center on condition that a board member oversee it for the first six months. Granddad wants you to do it."

"Me?" The question came out in a squeak. "But I—"

"You voted for it," Sam said, and disappeared.

Had she? She'd raised her hand for something. All she

remembered, somewhere between ghosts in Galveston and crime on the Caribbean, was the word *stipulation*.

Reluctantly, Tonya scooped up her bag and sat up. She wished she'd paid better attention. What kind of agency was Our Kids? "Uh, I'm not sure I'm, uh, qualified to supervise them," she said. No matter what Our Kids did, she was certain that was true. She wasn't qualified to supervise anything.

"Nonsense," Clint Brewster said, his tone implacable. "Janus will give you a list of guidelines. All you'll have to do is be sure the agency follows them."

Tonya felt a surge of relief. "You mean, drop in every now and then and check them out?" That she could probably handle.

Both her grandfather and Janus Nichols shook their heads. "You'll need to be on their premises," Nichols said.

Where were the premises? Frantically, Tonya glanced at Sam. Her cousin tapped a paper in front of her. Tonya scanned her own copy of the Our Kids Center proposal. An inner-city facility, dealing with predelinquent kids. What did she know about the inner city? What did she know about kids—predelinquent or otherwise?

"I'm, um, considering another job," she protested. The bookstore owner hadn't actually made an offer, but surely she would.

"But you haven't accepted yet," her grandfather said, his sharp eyes surveying her across the table.

"No, but—" Tonya glanced around the room. Surely one of the other board members would see that she was totally unsuitable for this job, and would say so. No one spoke. *Sam, help me out*, she pleaded silently. Her cousin remained disgustingly mute.

Tonya clenched her fists in her lap. She hated being pushed into anything she hadn't thought of herself. Trying for a tactful way to refuse the assignment, she said, "I don't believe I'm the person for the job. I wouldn't want to disappoint the foundation."

"You won't."

Why had she quit Desirée's? That job, which had bored her out of her mind last week, suddenly seemed appealing. She wondered if Desirée would take her back.

"You'll want to drive over this week and introduce yourself to the staff," Clint continued. "Janus will give you some more information after the meeting. Now, the next item on the agenda is..."

Tonya sighed. When Clint Brewster made up his mind, he was as unyielding as Texas granite. He hadn't turned a simple chili recipe into one of the largest food companies in the Southwest by being wishy-washy. She was stuck.

Or was she?

To placate the board she could visit Those Kids, or whatever it was called, and come back with solid evidence that she wasn't right for this position. Hard facts, that was what Clint liked. So she'd give them to him, embellish them if she had to. In fact, she'd enjoy outsmarting him. Warming to the challenge, she smiled to herself. She'd be out of this pickle in a week.

FEET POUNDING ON CEMENT, Kirk Butler drove the basketball down the court, then shot one-handed. The ball hovered for an instant on the basket's rim, then toppled through and hit the ground with a satisfying thump. Not satisfying enough. Kirk took the ball on the bounce, whirled and headed for the other end of the court. Although the weather had turned cool last night, sweat poured into his eyes and down the back of his neck, drenching his skin and his shirt. He approached the basket, leapt high and nailed another shot. When the ball fell into his hands, he tossed it hard against the backboard, caught it and hurled it again.

"You blowing off steam or trying to blast a hole in the wood?" asked a feminine voice behind him.

Kirk let the ball bounce past him. "Both."

A dark-skinned hand fell on his shoulder. "Rough morning," his friend Ladonna Martin surmised.

"Yeah." Kirk wiped the sweat from his eyes and stared down at his scuffed sneakers. "Rodney Hayes could've made it. I thought I'd convinced him, thought I had him sewed up. Then last night, the damn kid gets picked up for robbing a convenience store. Now he's headed for juvenile detention." With a vicious curse, Kirk grabbed the ball again and slammed it against the high chain-link fence that surrounded the basketball court.

Ladonna scrambled after the ball and tossed it back to Kirk. "Hurts to lose one."

"Especially one like this." Kirk tucked the basketball under his arm and the two walked in silence toward the side entrance of the OK Center.

As they approached the door, Ladonna said, "The Brewster Foundation called."

"Yeah?" For the first time that day, Kirk felt some of his anger and frustration drain. "What'd they say?"

"I don't know." Kirk opened the door and the two headed down the hallway toward the office. "Ramon took the call and I came out to get you."

In the office a muscular, dark-eyed man with longish black hair spoke into the phone. Ladonna took a chair and drummed her fingers on the desk. Kirk leaned against the wall and hooked a thumb through the belt loop of his jeans. His casual stance belied the tension building inside. Automatically, he rubbed his fingers over the silver buckle on his belt. If that grant from Brewster didn't come through...

Ramon Herrera's expression revealed nothing; neither did his end of the conversation, which consisted mainly of yes and no.

Finally he set the phone down. For a moment, he said nothing, letting the tension increase, then he raised his fist in a gesture of triumph. "Yes!"

"Hallelujah!" Ladonna leapt out of her chair and grabbed Ramon in an exuberant hug. "I knew we could do it." She grinned at him. "I knew *you* could do it. Your proposal won them over." Kirk nodded in agreement, and Ramon's cheeks flushed.

Kirk stepped forward and pumped his friend's arm. "Good work, buddy."

"Hey, we all worked," Ramon insisted. "Here's what they said. They'll fund us for a year at the rate we requested, then review our progress. If it's good, they'll back us for three more years." Cheers of approval sounded. He held up a hand for silence. "Now for the bad news. For the first six months they'll oversee us closely."

"Meaning?" Kirk said.

"Meaning a member of the Brewster board will be on-site—"

"Here?" Ladonna interrupted. "Breathing down our necks?"

"Yeah, well—"

"Is that standard?" Kirk asked, his brow furrowing.

"Depends on the foundation, but most of them are getting more cautious. A couple of years ago the Adams Foundation funded an agency that claimed to work with the elderly. Instead, the so-called directors pocketed half a million bucks."

"I see," Kirk said.

"But having someone here all the time, lookin' over our shoulders," Ladonna grumbled. "What's he gonna do?"

"She. She'll have an office in the building, watch what's going on. Someone from the family is coming. Name's Tonya Brewster." Ramon picked up a pencil, slid it casually between his fingers. "Nichols said she, um, majored in psychology in college."

"Oh well, then bring her on." Ladonna laid on the sarcasm as only she could.

"When'd she go to college?" Kirk asked.

"Yeah, in what century?" Ladonna added. "She was probably in class with Freud." She ran a hand over her tight curls and glanced at Kirk. "What are we going to do about this?"

"Well," Ramon offered uncertainly, "we *could* tell the Brewster Foundation to take their money and—" He finished the sentence with a crude description. "But are we in a position to do that?"

"Kirk, you haven't said anything. What do you think?" Ladonna asked, turning to him.

His gut reaction had been to tell the Brewster Foundation to take a hike, but that would be foolish. He couldn't spoil the center's chance to make a difference in this community, and he knew the others would listen to him. He erased the grim expression from his face and said, "Let's be sensible. We need the money, *bad.* I say we take it, give this Brewster lady an office and go on about our business. I guarantee she won't last here more than a week."

After a few token murmurs of protest, the others agreed. After all, as they all knew, they didn't have many choices.

"Okay, *compadres,*" Ramon said once that was settled. "Tonya Brewster wants to come for an inspection tour the day after tomorrow."

"So, go pretty up your offices," Ladonna ordered.

"Yeah. We also have a reporter from *Inside Texas* magazine coming that day to gather material for an article, *and* someone from the Houston schools made an appointment to talk about our summer programs. So let's make our offices *real* pretty."

"Got it," Ladonna said. "Hey, since we're about to become a funded facility, why don't we go out and do some celebrating after work?"

"Sounds good to me," Ramon said. "Pizza and beer?"

"Sure. Let's meet out front at six," Ladonna said. "Kirk?"

"I'm in. As long as we stick to the rules."

"No talking about work," the others chorused.

Kirk had instituted that rule soon after they'd started the Center, when he realized that they spent too many evenings rehashing daytime problems. Dinner out now was strictly fun and games. He liked the pizza joint they usually frequented. Small, crowded and convivial, it smelled of oregano and beer. The jukebox was loud, and the crowd, a mixture of blue-collar workers and professionals, even louder. He knew most of the regulars and had casually dated a few women he'd met there. He'd also indulged in a long-standing flirtation with one of the waitresses, who always managed to slip a few extra slices of pepperoni on his pizza.

Now, as the three of them left the conference room, Ladonna hesitated. "Since we're not talking about the center tonight, I've got one more question. Do you guys *really* think this is gonna work out?"

Ramon smiled, white teeth flashing against tan skin. "What Butler really thinks is that we don't need some rich bitch who doesn't know diddly squat about the streets coming in here to run the show."

He'd hit it squarely on the nose, but Kirk smiled easily. "Don't put words in my mouth, pal," he said. "That's what *you* think."

Ladonna's frown deepened. "You think she'll take over?"

"Nah." Kirk urged Ladonna out of the office and threw an arm around her shoulder. "No way some little blue-haired lady's gonna park herself here. She'll take one look at Janene North, fourteen and pregnant, and get a dose of Germain Parker's mouth, then head straight back to the country club."

"I surely hope so," Ladonna murmured.

"Count on it," Kirk assured her. "Miz Brewster will be here and gone so fast we won't even notice she's been around."

TONYA GLANCED at the scribbled directions on the slip of paper in her hand. Shaking her head, she pulled over and picked up the city map beside her. "Turn right on Magnolia," she muttered. "Where's Magnolia?" Squinting at the jumble of lines and tiny print that mapmakers seemed to delight in, she finally located the street. "Two more blocks."

She swung out into the street again, creeping along far below her usual speed so she wouldn't miss her turn. Taking her time gave her a chance to study the neighborhood. Debris-strewn gutters. Shabby apartment buildings decorated with graffiti. Run-down stores, several with benches in front occupied by surly-looking young men, lounging in the faint February sun as if they had nothing better to do. They eyed her with menacing interest as she drove past. Drug dealers? Carjackers? Tonya shivered.

Well, she wouldn't be here long. If her grandfather had any sense, he wouldn't *want* her here long. She'd stress that at dinner tonight. This neighborhood couldn't be safe.

And in case apprising him of the danger wasn't enough, she'd tour the center, take a few notes and explain that she had neither the interest nor the expertise to manage an inner-city facility. Nope, *her* talent was in...

Nothing, she admitted with a sudden pang. She wasn't an expert in much of anything except wanderlust.

Before she had time to reflect on her shortcomings, she spied the street sign she was looking for and made a right, glad to get off the main thoroughfare and away from the staring eyes.

Magnolia was a residential street. The name conjured up a vision of wide lawns, palatial homes, but these residences were shotgun houses, dilapidated bungalows with sagging porches and tiny, ill-kept yards. Only one or two showed evidence of care and pride—flower gardens, well-tended grass. The rest looked as if they should be bulldozed. Rusty pickups occupied several of the driveways. A chubby toddler dressed in denim overalls sat on the steps of one house. He waved as Tonya drove past.

Three blocks down she came upon the OK Center. The building, which looked as if it had once been a school, was brick, with a large central structure and wings fanning out on either side. The yard was clean, with none of the trash Tonya had seen littering the fronts of other buildings in the area. She saw a basketball court enclosed by a chain-link fence and, close to the building, playground equipment shaded by tall oak trees.

She pulled into a parking space and got out of her car. She started to lock it, then remembered the briefcase she'd brought. She opened the door, leaned over and reached across the front seat, then backed out.

"That car is begging to be stripped," growled a harsh voice in her ear.

Tonya gasped and turned to meet a pair of angry brown eyes.

She wished she'd taken the self-defense course Sam had

recommended, but even a black belt wouldn't help her take on this guy. He was big. Very big. Wide shoulders, massive chest. And those eyes. Fury leapt from them like sparks from an electric wire.

The thought flashed through her mind that this was just the scenario she might have concocted to convince her grandfather that she shouldn't be here. But she didn't care for the reality now staring her in the face.

Was the man a mugger? A rapist? Or just your ordinary car thief?

Though her heart pounded, Tonya refused to cringe. She forced herself to look him in the eye. "Wh-what do you want?" she whispered.

"Give me your keys and—"

Her keys? She'd give him her money, her watch, but not the keys to Rusty, her beloved Jaguar. Never. How dare he, and in broad daylight, too.

Frantically, Tonya glanced over her shoulder. A blue Chevy turned into a parking spot a few spaces down, and a tall, mahogany-skinned woman wearing a gray nylon jacket got out. Thank God!

Tonya mashed down the button on the tiny alarm box on her key ring. A high-pitched wail sounded, and the man jumped back.

"What the hell?" he roared, covering his ears.

"Help!" Tonya screamed, adding her voice to the din. "Help!"

She dashed around the back of the car with the brute right behind her. The pavement was uneven. She stumbled into a pothole and her shoe came off. Her briefcase slid out of her hand.

Like a character in an old Keystone Kops movie, her pursuer tripped over it and fell to his knees.

Tonya saw him go down, and unable to restrain her anger at his audacity, she raised her purse high in the air and brought it down on his head.

At that moment, the woman reached her. "Hey, what is it? What's going on?" she shouted, drowning out the curses issuing from the man's mouth.

"He...he tried to...steal my car." Gasping for breath, Tonya lifted her purse again.

"He..." The woman stared at the dark-eyed man, who was getting to his feet. "Kirk? You ripping off this lady's car?"

Hands up to protect his face from Tonya's wrath, the man shook his head. "Hell, no. I was about to offer to park it in the back for her when she went ballistic on me."

Silently, the three stared at one another. Lord, what had she done, Tonya thought. The poor guy had tried to be a hero, and she'd assaulted him with a designer handbag. "I, uh..."

Trying to think of a way out of this embarrassing situation, she stared at the man in front of her. He looked tough, disreputable. Shaggy chestnut hair reached his jacket collar, and even this early in the day his face bore a dark stubble, evidence of an indifferent shave. His jeans were frayed and faded, his shoes scuffed. The silver buckle at his waist looked like a lethal weapon in itself. He reminded her of a pirate, one of those impudent, reckless adventurers from the movies she'd watched as a kid. "How was I supposed to know what he wanted?" she mumbled. "He looks dangerous."

The woman laughed, a rich, throaty sound. "Yeah, he sure does," she agreed, "but he's really a pussycat."

Tonya doubted that. He might not be a mugger, but he was nobody's kitten. A tiger, more likely. But the humor of the situation struck her, and she, too, began to chuckle. After a moment, the man joined in. A dimple slashed his left cheek, and laughter transformed his face from threatening to wickedly appealing. She suddenly remembered that the pirates in those old movies were also always devilishly sexy.

The woman extended a hand. "I'm Ladonna Martin. Can I help you with something?"

Tonya shook her hand. "I'm Tonya Brewster. I have an appointment at the Our Kids Center."

"Well, you're here." Ladonna frowned. "Did you say Brewster?" When Tonya nodded, Ladonna shot a meaningful look at the man. "Well, Ms. Brewster," she said, her voice suddenly becoming sugary, "we're certainly glad to have you. This is Kirk Butler, one of our founders." Another glance at the man.

He was one of the center's founders? With an effort, Tonya kept her mouth from dropping open as she turned to shake his hand.

He'd extended it, all right, but he held out her shoe. "Oh," she mumbled, embarrassed again. She took the shoe, bent to slip it on, then looked up again.

His hand was still out. If her heart had pounded when she'd thought he was a carjacker, it beat double time now as she laid her hand in his. Strong, callused fingers grasped hers. He stared at her, and there was something in his gaze. Something very male, very...dangerous. Tonya swallowed.

Behind her, she heard the soft clearing of a throat. At the sound, the gleam in Kirk Butler's eyes disappeared, to be replaced by a look of cool appraisal.

Confused, Tonya pulled her hand away. His remained extended. "Keys," he said.

"The car'll be safer in the back," Ladonna urged.

Reluctantly, Tonya handed over her keys. Kirk Butler's hand closed around them, then, without another word, he strode back to Tonya's car.

2

TONYA DIDN'T SEE HIM again when she went inside. Although the center's other founders—Ladonna and Ramon Herrera—joined her in Ramon's office, Kirk didn't put in an appearance. Tonya told herself she was relieved. That powerful male aura would have distracted her, and she needed to concentrate on what was being said as well as pretend she understood it.

Besides that, something was wrong here. Although both Ladonna and Ramon sounded enthusiastic and friendly, she sensed it was a sham. When they didn't realize she was looking at them, she saw the same cool dislike in their eyes that she'd seen in Kirk's. Why? she wondered. She'd expected them to be delighted about the foundation's support. Instead, she felt an undercurrent of hostility hidden behind false smiles.

Ramon, who served as the center's administrator, went over the current budget and showed Tonya the new programs they would initiate once the funding was in place. As he spoke, she nodded and made notes. She'd never dealt with figures this large. How was she supposed to oversee this kind of money? Not only would she have to get past animosity she didn't understand, but she'd be way over her head coping with financial matters.

Ramon leaned forward. "One thing we're going to concentrate on is our mentoring program. Kirk Butler, our program director, will tell you more about that when you meet him."

"We've, um, met," Tonya said. Ladonna coughed, probably to cover a laugh, and Tonya's cheeks heated.

Apparently unaware of the byplay, Ramon continued. "We have a good start, but we need to recruit more successful men to give these boys role models, show them they can have another future besides hanging out in a gang."

"What about a program for girls?" Tonya asked.

"Sure. The girls need mentors, too," Ladonna said, and Tonya thought she saw a flicker of respect in the woman's eyes.

"The grant will allow us to hire several new staff members," Ramon continued. "And we hope the foundation can help us with community contacts and publicity."

"Contacts," Tonya murmured. She scribbled another note and cringed inwardly. These people wanted big corporate contacts, and she doubted the owner of a boutique or a mystery bookstore would count.

When the meeting ended, Ladonna said, "I'll take you on a tour."

As they left Ramon's office, Tonya noticed her car keys on the front desk. Kirk Butler had apparently brought them in and left. Although she reminded herself that she was glad he hadn't attended the meeting, she couldn't help but wonder why. Following Ladonna down the hall, she put Kirk out of her mind and tried to concentrate on what the woman was saying.

"This neighborhood is ethnically mixed and that makes for a volatile situation. Fifteen, twenty years ago the area was white, but then African Americans started moving in and, later, Hispanics. Each race has its own gangs, and believe me, some of what goes on between them, you don't

vanna know. About the only time those kids see eye to eye
is when we get 'em together for sports."

They stopped at a small room, empty except for a black
metal desk and a couple of chairs. The walls, however,
made up for the scarcity of furnishings. Bright posters,
snapshots of children, kids' crayon drawings covered every
available inch of space. "Nice," Tonya said.

"Thanks. I like to have color around. Makes me feel
happy." Ladonna hung her jacket over the back of her
chair, then deposited her purse in the desk drawer and
locked it. "You gotta keep your valuables locked up
around here. Don't want to tempt the kids. They got
enough temptation other places. We'll get you a desk with
a key. You going to be starting here Monday?"

"I don't know," Tonya answered honestly. "Maybe, or
maybe someone else from the foundation will. I have
some...other commitments."

She heard a sound behind her and turned to see Kirk
lounging in the doorway, his eyes assessing her.

"I'm taking Tonya around the building," Ladonna began. The phone rang. She picked it up, listened a moment
and asked her caller to wait. Her hand over the mouth-
piece, she said, "It's Janene North's mother. This'll take a
while."

"That's all ri—" Tonya began.

"I'll show you around," Kirk interrupted, his eyes crin-
kling with mirth, "as long as you promise not to beat me
with your purse."

Tonya felt a blush stain her cheeks. Reluctantly, she
joined him in the hall.

Though at five-seven she was taller than average, she felt
like a pygmy walking beside a giant. He had to be at least
six foot four, and every inch of it male muscle. His stride
was long. She practically had to jog to keep up with him. In-

tending to look businesslike this morning, she'd worn her one and only suit, and its pencil-slim skirt didn't allow for sprinting down hallways. Or sprinting anywhere, as she'd found out earlier when she'd tripped in the pothole. Any minute now the skirt would rip or she'd trip in her high heels. "Could you slow down?" she panted.

He complied without apology. "You'd better wear jeans next time you're here," he suggested, then glanced at her sharply. "But you're not sure you're coming back, are you?"

Was that a hopeful note in his voice? Chagrined that he'd overheard her remark to Ladonna, Tonya shook her head.

"You ought to think it over," he said.

Tonya halted in midstride. "Why?"

"I don't imagine this is your usual kind of hangout. The neighborhood's rough, this place is rough."

She'd had the same thought herself when she'd driven into the area, but hearing him say it miffed her. "I can take care of myself."

"Think that purse would hold off a gang?"

She wished he'd leave her purse out of it. His voice was teasing, but the scornful look in his eyes piqued her temper even further.

Before she could think of a cutting reply, he turned, unlocked a door and waved her inside a room furnished with desks, bookshelves and a couple of beanbag chairs. "This is our after-school study hall," he said.

Tonya glanced at the meager supplies on the shelves. A couple of dictionaries, an atlas, a dog-eared encyclopedia. She'd noticed a number of items on their to-buy list that must have been intended for this room.

As they continued down the hall, Tonya heard children's voices. Now Kirk opened a door painted bright yellow and they entered a large, sunny room filled with a dozen children, ranging from infants to preschoolers. Walls the same cheery yellow as the door were decorated with nursery rhyme characters. Here the shelves overflowed with toys. In the middle of the room, two toddlers fought over a stuffed animal, in one corner a sad-looking youngster sat with his thumb in his mouth, and in another corner a woman crooned to an infant as she changed him.

Puzzled, Tonya turned to Kirk. "I thought you worked with older kids."

"These are the children of some of those older kids."

"The children?" she echoed.

"Teenage pregnancy. Around here it's almost a badge of honor."

"Oh," she muttered.

"New world for you, huh?" he said.

Of course it was, but that didn't mean she couldn't learn to fit in. Provided she wanted to. Which, she reminded herself, she didn't.

They left the nursery and visited a workshop, an auditorium, a games room with table tennis and a pool table, and a kitchen, where the smell of coffee drifted to Tonya's nostrils. "Want a cup?" Kirk asked. He sounded impatient, as if he was eager to end the tour and get back to whatever he had to do.

Obstinately, she decided to accept his offer. "Yes, thanks." He poured her a cup and came close to hand it to her. Too close. Tonya took a step back.

Kirk moved forward and stopped, one arm resting on the wall beside her. "So, what do you think?" he asked.

"I think the center has potential."

"I meant, are you planning to come back?"

He clearly hoped she wasn't. She ought to take on the job, just to show him she could do it. She lifted her chin. "You heard me earlier. I haven't decided."

"You'd better ditch the Jag if you do. That buggy won't last a day around here."

"Different car, different clothes." She couldn't keep the sarcasm from her voice. "Maybe I should cut my hair, too."

"No." His fingers grazed the ends of her hair, and though she barely felt their touch, Tonya shivered. For a moment they stared at each other, neither of them moving or speaking. Then Kirk dropped his hand, and his eyes, which had darkened from brown to black, turned cool again.

To distract herself from the confusing feelings his touch engendered, Tonya groped for the anger she'd felt earlier. "You're trying to talk me out of coming," she accused.

He shrugged. "Why would I do that?"

"You tell me," she challenged.

"Okay, I'll be straight with you," he said, moving fractionally closer.

She felt the heat of his body, saw the pulse in his throat. For a moment, she felt like a defenseless animal, caught in the gaze of a sleek, predatory tiger. She wanted to shrink back, but she caught herself. Instead, she stared at him coolly. "Do that."

His mouth hardened. "This isn't the country club. You walk out the door here, you run into crack dealers, gangs, maybe a teenage girl selling herself for drug money."

Tonya swallowed, but she refused to let him unnerve her. "So?"

"So maybe you don't belong here."

"You don't know that. Besides, it's my decision."

He shrugged again. "Right."

Abruptly, Tonya stepped around him and set down the untasted coffee. "Thanks for the tour," she said over her shoulder as she headed for the door. Kirk followed her out of the kitchen and fell into step beside her as she hurried down the hall. "I can find my way out," she told him, her voice still frosty.

He pulled a set of keys out of his pocket, tossed them up and caught them. "Back parking lot's kept locked."

She'd have to endure his company for another few minutes, she thought crossly, keeping her eyes forward. She wouldn't stare at those muscular arms, wouldn't speculate about how those blunt fingers might feel on her skin. Why should she? She didn't like Kirk Butler at all.

But as she drove out of the parking lot a few minutes later, she was appalled to find herself watching him in the rearview mirror as he relocked the gate. All right, nothing was wrong with appreciating a healthy male animal, she told herself, as long as you didn't venture too close. She didn't intend to do that, even though she'd be working side by side with him at the OK Center.

Tonya blinked. Working...where?

Here.

Somewhere between the kitchen and her car, she'd made her decision. As of Monday morning, she'd be the Brewster in residence here. The center staff—and Kirk in particular—would just have to get used to it.

KIRK STALKED into the building and down the hall to Ramon's office, where Ramon and Ladonna were meeting over brown-bag lunches. He sat down and snitched a handful of potato chips from Ladonna.

She batted his hand away. "How'd the grand tour go?"

He shrugged. "She hasn't made up her mind about coming back."

"What do you think she's gonna decide?"

Kirk scowled and grabbed another chip. "Who knows?"

"Whatever she does, we'll still get the money, won't we?" Ladonna asked with a worried frown.

"Sure," Ramon said.

"Maybe they'll send someone more...appropriate," Ladonna offered, then held out a newspaper clipping. "I found this in Monday's *Express* when I put the papers out for recycling." She cleared her throat. "'Tonya Brewster, wearing a minidress by Ar-Armani...'" She looked up. "What the heck is Armani? Sounds like a pasta dish." Then she continued. "'Was seen enjoying the music at the annual fund-raiser for the Cystic Fibrosis Foundation at the Ritz Carlton.'"

Ramon snatched the article and let out a long, low whistle. "*Mamacita!* Look at those legs."

He tossed the paper to Kirk, who took it reluctantly. He'd already had an eye-popping view of Tonya Brewster's legs when he'd been on his knees in the pothole, and the vivid picture had imprinted itself firmly on his mind. He also had a clear memory of the silkiness of her long dark hair, the exotic fragrance of the perfume she wore. And he hated it.

Ramon peered at the article again over Kirk's shoulder. "That's some blue-haired lady."

Kirk balled the paper up and tossed it in the trash. "She looks like a damn centerfold," he muttered.

"Prom queen," Ladonna corrected.

"Whatever."

"What's eatin' you?" Ramon asked, gazing at Kirk with narrowed eyes. "You usually go for that type."

"Not here. This is business." Frustrated, Kirk glanced around the room. "We'd be a lot better off if she looked like we expected. Can't you see what kind of problems she'll cause?"

Blank gazes met his. Then Ladonna said, "Yeah, the boys—"

"Right. One look at her and their hormones are gonna

kick in big time." He sighed. "And if *she* doesn't stir them up, her car will."

"Jaguar," Ladonna said appreciatively. "Fire engine red. Mmm-*mmm*."

"Yeah?" Ramon's eyes lit up.

"See?" Kirk said. "Even you two could get whipped into a frenzy over the car." He glanced at Ramon with narrowed eyes. *Not to mention Tonya herself.*

"Maybe I should talk to her," Ladonna mused. "You know, woman to woman."

"I already told her to find a different set of wheels if she comes back," Kirk said. "And to wear jeans." He didn't add that he'd told her she didn't belong here.

"Hey, let's look on the bright side," Ramon suggested. "They could have sent somebody worse."

Ladonna nodded. "Some Pollyanna type who wants to rehabilitate the dear little children of the ghetto."

Ramon tossed his lunch bag in the trash and leaned back in his chair. "She'll be okay. And like Kirk said the other day, she'll be out of our hair before too long."

Hair, Kirk thought. Back in the kitchen, he'd itched to comb his fingers through her hair, bury his face in it. He'd had to force himself to drop his hand.

After lunch, he marched back to his office and slammed the door behind him. Instead of sitting down to work, he stood at the window, staring out at the yard without seeing anything. He hadn't felt this restless, this edgy, in a long time. Anger simmered in his veins. Anger at *her*. Finding a calm space for himself, finding the calm inside himself hadn't been easy. Now she was going to disrupt his life. And he was frustrated with himself because he wouldn't be able to prevent it.

His eyes finally focused on the empty basketball court, then on the ball that lay in the corner of his office. He needed to let out some of that anger. He grabbed the ball and started outside.

Ramon and Ladonna still believed what he'd said the other day, that Tonya wouldn't last long here. But they hadn't seen what he had—the look of stubbornness that had appeared on that pretty face. He sighed. Six months of supervision, the Brewster Foundation had stipulated. He had a feeling, with Tonya Brewster around, he would be shooting a lot of baskets in the next six months.

"OUCH! BEHAVE YOURSELF." Tonya shook her finger at the kitten, who had sunk his sharp little claws into her leg. Kneeling, she picked him up and rubbed his tummy.

The kitten unsheathed his claws again and growled.

"You're a tough one, aren't you?" Tonya rolled him over on his back.

Instantly, the kitten turned over and sprang to his feet, his back arched high. When Tonya made no move, he crouched and stared at her.

"You little tiger," she said, and her thoughts returned to Kirk. Ladonna had called him a pussycat, but in Tonya's mind, he too was a tiger. She grinned. "I think I'll call you Butler." She scooped up the kitten, put him in the utility room and shut the door. She'd better hurry or she'd be late for dinner at her grandparents'.

After a ten-minute search for her car keys, she dashed out, her watch telling her she had only a few minutes until dinnertime. Nevertheless, when she passed a florist with a sign in the window advertising spring blooms, she couldn't resist stopping to buy a bouquet of delicate purple irises. Her grandmother loved flowers.

She arrived only fifteen minutes late—a record. When she pulled into the circular drive in front of her grandparents' graceful white antebellum mansion, she saw that Sam and Wade had already arrived. Sam's new husband had a penchant for punctuality. In fact, he'd taken to calling Tonya "Rabbit," telling her she reminded him of the White Rabbit in *Alice in Wonderland*. He'd even taken to singing to her, "I'm late, I'm late, for a very important date," when the urge struck. Tonya hoped he'd forgo the concert tonight.

She breezed into the living room and bestowed kisses and apologies all around. "I hope dinner isn't ruined," she told her grandmother as she handed her the flowers.

Martha Brewster exclaimed over the bouquet and shook her head. "I always plan meals late when you're coming, dear."

"How'd your visit to Our Kids go?" Clint asked as Tonya sat on the couch.

She decided to omit mentioning the incident with the car. "The staff was polite, but they didn't exactly welcome me with open arms."

"I'm not surprised," her grandfather said. "I'm sure they don't like the strings we've attached to the grant, but they have no choice. They don't have a track record. They've only been in operation a couple of years. I'm not willing to give them a blank check until they prove their worth to me." He sipped his bourbon. "You'll need to show them you're not there to run the place, just to keep an eye on them."

"I intend to."

Her grandfather nodded, looking pleased.

Across the room, Sam's eyes widened. Not surprising. Only yesterday Tonya had told her she had no intention of working at the OK Center. Tonya gave her a bland smile before she turned back to her grandfather. "I'll need a different car."

"Good idea," Wade Phillips said. "That neighborhood has one of the highest crime rates in the city. Kids over there don't stop at stealing hubcaps." He stretched his long legs in front of him and grinned lazily at Tonya. "I'm thinking of trading my little Toyota pickup for a new one. I could hold on to it and let you use it if you could stand driving it after getting used to a Jag."

"I guess it won't kill me."

He grinned. "It's a deal, then." More serious now, he continued, "You have to be careful in that neighborhood, you know. Keep your doors locked. Drive in the center lane. That way, you're not as likely to get forced off the road. Do you still have that alarm I gave you?" When she nodded, he added, "Check the battery."

Tonya smiled to herself. The battery worked just fine.

"If anyone approaches you, use it."

She didn't mention that she already had, with interesting results.

Later, after dinner, Sam pulled Tonya aside. "I thought you were dead set against working at that agency. What made you change your mind?"

"The challenge."

Sam raised a brow.

"They don't want me there."

"You heard what Granddad said. They wouldn't want anyone there."

"No, it's me specifically."

"You can't take this personally," Sam began, then turned as her husband came up and put an arm around her shoulder. For a moment, she seemed to forget what she was about to say as she gazed into Wade's eyes.

Tonya felt a flash of envy. She often forgot what she was going to say, but not for such a romantic reason; she just lost her train of thought.

Sam blinked, then said, "Tonya thinks the people at the Our Kids Center dislike her personally."

"Well, one of them in particular. He...he was just so antagonistic. He told me I didn't belong there."

"Want me to beat him up?" Wade offered.

Tonya grinned. "Yeah. No, maybe not. He looks pretty tough even for you. He's big." She spread her arms. "Really big—"

"Brass knuckles should do it."

"And predatory."

"Ah," Sam said, watching her. "A bad boy. He sounds intriguing."

Tonya didn't comment on that.

"Why don't you hang on a week before you have Wade beat him up," Sam suggested. "See if you can tame him first."

"Good idea," Tonya said, then chuckled. "I named my cat after him. Butler. Kirk Butler."

"Butler," Wade muttered. "Name sounds familiar."

Tonya tossed her hair back as they walked into the living room. "You probably heard it from one of your...what do you call informants? Stoolies? Someone at the state prison."

Wade burst out laughing. "Poor guy. You're gonna give him a hard time, Rabbit."

"Yep," Tonya said. "I expect I will."

THE NEXT MORNING when she called the OK Center, Kirk Butler answered the phone. She recognized his distinctive growl immediately. "Good morning. This is Tonya Brewster," she said.

"Yes."

He sounded as if he had no idea who she was. She could answer in the same impersonal tone, but she was determined to win these people over, even the tiger. "How are you, Kirk?" she asked brightly.

"Um, fine."

Surprised I recognized your voice, aren't you? "I wanted to let you know I'll be starting Monday."

"You decided to come, then?"

She couldn't tell from his voice how he felt about her statement...but she could guess. She smiled to herself. "If you'll remind Ramon that I'll need an office—"

"I'll take care of it."

"Thanks. See you Monday."

She hung up and scooped up the cat, who purred noisily, then opened the door of her closet. "He won't believe it when I drive up, kitty."

No more classy Jaguar. She'd drive Wade's pickup. And no more nine-to-five suit. She surveyed her wardrobe and made her choice: a slightly faded T-shirt from Caneel Bay Resort in the Virgin Islands and a pair of designer jeans with a strategic tear at the knee. With a satisfied smile, she tossed the clothes on the dresser. She'd fit right in at the OK Center.

3

SHE'D NEVER FIT IN HERE, Kirk thought as he stood at his window and watched Tonya lug two bags into the building. She'd driven a pickup today; though it was a two-year-old model, it still looked spanking new. She'd worn jeans and a T-shirt but they were designer duds, and she still carried that damn purse with those interlocking Cs that shouted, "Cold cash." Not only were her clothes too fancy, but those damn jeans clung as if they'd been spray painted on. And the T-shirt...that didn't even bear thinking about.

He wondered what she carried in those paper bags. Something for her office, no doubt. An elaborate leather desk set worth as much as his paycheck. Or a brass nameplate for the door. He knew he was being petty, but he couldn't seem to help it. He let out a breath and stepped back from the window. The best way to deal with the irritation she evoked, he concluded, was to avoid her.

Even so, he found himself thinking about her as the morning progressed, wondering what she was doing, inventing reasons to stroll past her office. The first time, he glanced inside and saw that the room was empty. One of the paper bags lay on the desk with notebooks, pencils, a dictionary and other office supplies spilling out of it. When he passed by again later, the door was shut, but he heard the sound of laughter, male and female. He loitered at the water fountain, read and reread the notices on the hallway bulletin board, and cursed his curiosity. At last the door opened and Ramon ambled out, his face wreathed with a smile.

He saw Kirk and raised a hand in greeting. Kirk didn't return the greeting or the smile.

"Classy lady," Ramon remarked as he continued toward the front of the building.

So she'd already charmed one of the staff.

"I invited her to join us at the Rotary Club banquet this evening. She was impressed when I told her we were getting an award."

Oh, hell. Having her around all day was bad enough. Now he'd have to endure the evening with her, too. If he weren't giving the acceptance speech, he'd skip the banquet. Kirk realized his hand had balled into a fist. Abruptly, he murmured an excuse to Ramon, swung around and stalked back to his office.

He managed to keep out of Tonya's way the rest of the day. When he glanced out his window and saw the pickup drive off late in the afternoon, he breathed a heavy sigh. At least he could relax until time for the banquet. Maybe she wouldn't come, he thought hopefully.

But he knew she would. Okay, he'd say hello, be polite and cool. No fraternizing with the Brewster elite.

Later as he strode down the hall, he saw that she'd left her office door open. He slowed as he went by, then stopped in the doorway of the now cluttered room. Damned if he couldn't smell her perfume. Even though she'd been gone a good half hour, the musky, exotic scent lingered and teased his nostrils. It made him think of a hot, humid night, thick with the fragrance of jasmine. He imagined a garden steeped in moonlight, a woman in his arms, her hair flowing over his fingers, her lips moist and open under his. *Tonya*, he thought, then cursed viciously.

"*¿Qué pasa?*"

Kirk started at Ramon's voice. He hadn't even noticed the other man come up beside him. *What's going on? Nothing except that I'm losing my mind.* "Just remembered something I have to take care of." He continued down the hall.

Ramon fell into step beside him. "Tonya seems to be settling in just fine. She wants to get together with everyone and go over the specific programs each person's handling. She gave me a list. You're first."

Damn! So much for keeping out of her way. "When's the meeting?" Kirk asked.

"Tomorrow. She said she has a couple things to take care of first. She'll meet with you in your office at ten—"

He could summarize his programs quickly, get her out of his way by ten-thirty, eleven at the latest.

"And then spend the rest of the day with you, observing."

"The day! She wants to spend the whole damn day?" Tonight, tomorrow, six months. When would he get her out of his hair?

Ramon nodded. "What's the problem? You've had observers here before."

But not her. "No big deal," Kirk said quickly. "I'm busy, that's all."

"Hey, *amigo*, for the amount of money Brewster's giving us, you can be less busy for a day."

"Right," Kirk said without conviction.

Ramon put a hand on Kirk's shoulder. "I know you don't like her, but try not to let it show."

"No problem." With an effort, Kirk controlled a laugh. What he didn't like was his extraordinary reaction to her. He was no better than the teenagers who came to the center. His hormones were raging out of control, and he hoped he could keep *that* from showing.

There'd been plenty of women in his life but only one

who'd mattered. And even with Amelia he hadn't felt this instant attraction, this frantic craving. Their relationship had developed over time. They'd met in an English class their junior year in college. She was the sorority girl; no matter that he was a product of the inner city, he was the football hero, then an NFL draft pick. They'd been the perfect couple. Until his professional football career had ended in an explosion of pain after only one game. And when it was clear he'd become an *ex*-football hero, Amelia had dropped him—just when he'd needed her most.

No, he didn't want another Amelia, another spoiled rich debutante. He'd been careful to confine his relationships— if his short-term involvements could be termed relationships—to women who weren't from the country club set. And he intended to keep it that way. Unfortunately, his libido didn't seem to be getting the message.

THE ROTARY CLUB BANQUET was held at a Holiday Inn near the downtown area. Tonya stopped at the desk and got directions for the ballroom. Inside, she glanced around, looking for the group from the OK Center. She spotted Kirk immediately. Head and shoulders above the rest, he stood in the center of a circle of men and women.

God, he looked gorgeous. Gone were the ragged jeans and scruffy sneakers. Tonight he wore an impeccably tailored navy blue suit, crisp white shirt and patterned tie. A disguise, she thought. Although he could pass for a corporate executive this evening, he couldn't quite conceal the sexy pirate that lurked beneath the polished facade. As she walked toward him, Tonya's pulse accelerated.

He turned, glanced around the room and saw her. Tonya smiled and waved. Kirk responded with a nod. He didn't even return her smile, but his eyes traveled over her as if he were assessing every inch of her outfit...and what was underneath. He wasn't the first man who'd undressed her with his eyes, but he was the first to whom she'd reacted so strongly. She felt a mixture of excitement, trepidation and pleasure—a jumble of emotions that thoroughly confused her.

She forced herself to look away from Kirk and search for the rest of the OK Center staff. She spied Ladonna, attired in a gold knit dress, deep in conversation with a middle-aged man in a brown suit. And Ramon, standing with his arm around a petite brunette. He saw Tonya and waved.

When she reached them, Ramon introduced her first to his wife, Elena, then to several of the Rotarians. Tonya acknowledged the introductions, greeted Ladonna, and glanced at Kirk. He didn't speak. Well, she could remedy that. She marched straight over to him. "Kirk, how are you?" she asked.

His expression didn't change, but at least she'd forced him to acknowledge her. "Fine. Glad you could make it."

Liar, Tonya thought, and flashed him a brilliant smile, then began a conversation with the gentleman beside her. She was used to the social scene, comfortable with it, and she had no trouble mixing with the Rotarians and their guests. As she did, she was conscious of Kirk watching her.

Surreptitiously, she observed him, too. He surprised her. One of the men in the group asked if he was following the Dawson case, the trial of a high-profile land developer accused of poisoning his wife that had made daily headlines in the Houston *Express*.

"The prosecutor has a mountain of evidence, but it's all circumstantial," Kirk said, and proceeded to discuss the case in detail. Tonya heard snatches of his conversation and realized how articulate he was.

She wouldn't have thought him a social kind of guy, but he was smooth and self-assured in this group of businesspeople. Of course, he could have no confidence at all and still score with the women. Even though many were a good ten or even twenty years his senior, they fluttered around him, blushing like schoolgirls at his every glance.

At dinner, he sat one table over from her, but she could tell when he looked her way because the hair on the back of her neck prickled.

Dinner consisted of standard banquet fare—green salad, chicken, green beans, rolls. Tonya wondered why the restaurant chef didn't dress up the food a bit with some kind of zippy sauce for the chicken or a different vegetable. Dessert was also predictable—white cake with chocolate frosting. She supposed the after-dinner speeches would be equally bland.

She was wrong.

When the award was presented to the Our Kids Center for "making a difference" in their neighborhood, Tonya was surprised to see Kirk, rather than Ramon, rise to accept it.

He thanked the Rotary Club for the award, then said, "I want to tell you a story. It's about a boy named Daniel, a young boy, nine years old. He was just a child, really, but he'd already experienced many things no child should...."

Tonya sat listening, mesmerized by his words, by the emotion with which they were spoken, as he told the story. The circumstances were typical of youngsters growing up in the ghetto, and no doubt the audience, like Tonya, had heard dozens of similar stories. But Kirk made this account so touching, so true, that the youngster and his world came alive for everyone in the room. When he spoke of what the OK Center had done to turn young Daniel's life around, Tonya felt like cheering.

"And on behalf of the Our Kids Center, I thank you for this award and for the support you've given us since we began. With your continued help and that of others, we will keep on making a difference in the lives of young people and their families. Thank you."

Silence filled the ballroom for a moment, then the audience broke into loud and enthusiastic applause. No wonder they'd chosen Kirk to give the acceptance speech. No one could have been more dynamic.

When the program ended, one of the Rotary vice presidents invited the group from the center for a drink at the hotel bar to celebrate the award. Several other Rotarians joined them. The hostess at the bar had two tables pushed together to accommodate all twelve of them.

Tonya found herself crowded in next to Kirk. "I enjoyed your talk," she said.

"Thanks."

They stared at each other in uncomfortable silence for a moment, then turned away.

Tonya struck up a conversation with the couple across from her and soon had them laughing at her account of a recent trip to Mexico.

A combo began to play, and Ramon and his wife left the table to dance. Several others followed. Tonya danced with the Rotary vice president, with Ramon, with an elderly man who'd come alone.

But not with Kirk.

When he turned in her direction, she leaned toward him and murmured, "Don't you dance?"

"Yeah," he answered.

"Well then..."

"I like to do the asking."

Bastard. She raised her chin. "Be my guest," she muttered, and turned her back. "Tell me the history of the Rotary Club," she said, smiling at the man on her other side.

Tonya concentrated on the Rotarian, trying not to notice

the feel of Kirk's jacket brushing her shoulder, the scent of his aftershave, the sound of his voice. Trying not to notice which women he *asked* to dance.

Then his hand touched her shoulder, and she jumped. She turned and met his eyes. "Dance with me," he said.

"That sounds more like telling than asking."

But she rose and followed him to the small dance floor. When they faced each other, she gave him a teasing smile. "I guess you expect to lead, too."

"Yeah," he said, and flashed that quick, captivating grin.

The moment he put his arms around her, she knew she'd made a mistake agreeing to dance with him. His arms held her too firmly; his body was too hard, too masculine; his face was too close. He was the kind of man who made a woman go trembly inside, not the kind with whom she could establish a working relationship.

Her body aligned with his, Tonya seemed to float to the music. She forgot where she was and why she was there and thought only of Kirk. He led, but not the way she'd anticipated. She'd expected a big, tough guy like him to dominate on the dance floor. Instead, he guided her so smoothly, so expertly that she barely noticed he was in control.

When the song ended and he let her go, she blinked and glanced around in confusion. She felt as if she'd awakened from a dream.

Now reality set in, and with it came a question.

Managing all the details involved with overseeing the OK Center would be hard enough. How was she going to manage her attraction to Kirk Butler at the same time?

TONYA PARKED THE PICKUP in front of the OK Center and walked slowly inside. Butterflies danced in her stomach. Yesterday she'd felt confident and enthusiastic. Yesterday she'd only had to unpack her office supplies. Today was another matter.

She'd awakened early and spent an hour alternating between pacing her living room and making lists. Now she had to finish straightening her office, hook up her computer and meet with Kirk. Scheduling him before the other directors had been a good idea. Get the tough items over with first. Kirk Butler was tough.

They'd danced one dance in silence last night. Then he'd taken her back to the table, and they hadn't spoken for the rest of the evening. But the silence had been emotionally charged. Tonya had felt the electricity as surely as if she'd stuck her finger in a socket.

But this was another day, a workday, and she'd forget the way she'd felt in his arms last night. She'd concentrate on her job. Only trouble was, the job made her almost as nervous as Kirk did. *Someday, Grandfather, I'll get you for this.*

It was nearly ten-thirty when she hurried down the hall to Kirk's office. She'd gotten involved arranging and rearranging things in her office and forgotten the time.

She took a deep breath as she knocked on his door. Did her nervousness show? Of course not, she reassured herself. Kirk might be intimidating but he didn't read minds. He wouldn't see nerves because he wouldn't expect them. *She* was in charge here.

"Come in," he called, and she pushed open the door.

"Good morning," she said.

He nodded to a chair and glanced at his watch. The word *sorry* was on her lips, but she forced it back. Apologizing would give him the upper hand, and she refused to begin that way. She sat down and crossed her legs. "I want to familiarize myself with the programs here, get a rundown on everyone's responsibilities." Pleased with her businesslike start, she opened the notebook she'd brought.

"My title is program director," Kirk said. "One thing I handle is boys' athletics, with the help of James Watson, who's a coach at Jefferson Middle School," he continued, while she made notes. "Right now we're into basketball. We've divided the kids into teams that play each other. And I'm working on setting up a league with some other centers..."

He had a deep, gravelly voice, a voice that reminded her of a foreign film she'd once rented. It had contained the most sensual love scene she could remember. A dark room, the lovers no more visible than shadows. You couldn't see them, but you could hear the woman's soft sighs and the man's voice, rough and sexy like Kirk's, telling her what he wanted to do, what he *was* doing. And how he would do it all over again....

"This afternoon."

"Hmm?"

"I said, I guess you'll want to watch practice this afternoon."

"Oh, yes." With an effort, she brought herself back to the present. Carefully, she wrote "afternoon practice" in her notebook. "What time?"

"Four."

She wrote that down, too. "What else do you do?"

"When I'm not coaching, I work with the boys' club that meets every day after school. It's a way to keep these kids off the streets. We have activities for them like table tennis and other games, we take them on field trips, oversee their homework and tutor them if they need it. I spend a lot of time trying to recruit volunteers."

"Any success?" Tonya asked.

"Some, but not enough." He rubbed his chin in a gesture

of frustration. "I'd like to get some off-duty cops in here, show the boys the police aren't the enemy, demonstrate to the cops that these kids have potential, but so far all I've gotten is a cold shoulder."

Tonya wrote that down. Cops. She knew a lot of cops and she had the traffic tickets to prove it. Maybe she could recruit some of them.... "Could you give me some of your stationery, please?" she asked.

Kirk reached in his desk drawer and handed her several sheets. His fingers brushed hers. The touch lasted no longer than a heartbeat, but Tonya had to stifle a gasp.

She glanced up. He was watching her. Amid the hard planes and angles of his face, his eyes were beautiful, a rich, liquid brown and so deep they seemed fathomless. Caught in his hypnotic gaze, she set the pen down. She felt her fingers tremble. Why was he staring at her so intently?

Then he blinked and the brief spell was broken. She let out a deep breath. She'd had something she wanted to say, but it escaped her. Fighting to control her breathing, she stared at the stationery she still clutched and said the first thing that came into her mind. "You need a new letterhead. Something colorful, maybe with little stick figures of kids."

"We don't have money to waste on stationery."

"But the grant—"

"Won't go for frills," he said. "We need to beef up our programs, hire more staff."

Tonya swallowed at his harsh tone and cast around for another subject. "Do you, um, have a job program?"

"Yeah, for the older kids, but many of the children we work with are too young for after-school jobs." His voice was even. Tonya wondered if he'd already forgotten the charged look that had passed between them, or if she'd imagined it. "Even if they could get jobs," he continued, "there'd be a problem."

She tried to match his tone. "What?"

"The jobs they'd qualify for aren't attractive to them."

"Why?" Tonya asked, interested now. "I'd think they would be delighted to make a little money."

"That's the problem. A *little* money doesn't appeal to these kids. They see their older brothers raking in dough with very little effort—"

"I don't understand," Tonya said. "Raking in dough doing what?"

"Dealing drugs," Kirk answered. "Plenty of junior crack pushers are the sole support of their families."

Of course. She should have realized that. "And my sixteen-year-old cousin works at McDonald's."

His eyes turned cool. "Yeah, your cousin's learning responsibility, but we're talking survival here. Your cousin doesn't have an absent father, a mother who lies around the house half-drunk all the time and a landlord breathing down his neck."

Neatly put in her place, Tonya nodded.

"Sorry," Kirk said. "Trying to yank these kids out of a vicious cycle is frustrating. So many factors come into play...." His voice trailed off.

Tonya watched him, the earnest expression on his hard face, the fisted hand. She could feel the intensity, the passion when he spoke about his work. "You really care about the kids you work with," she murmured.

"Sure I do," he said, his voice suddenly cold. "I was one of them."

Shocked, Tonya stared at him. "You grew up in a neighborhood like this?"

"Two blocks from here. All of us did." When she remained silent, he said, "Surprised, Ms. Brewster, that real human beings live here, not statistics?"

She slapped her notebook down on his desk and glared

at him. "Yes, I'm surprised. I don't know your background." As she spoke, her temper flared higher. "I'd have been just as surprised if you'd said you grew up on Park Avenue." She shoved back her chair and stood. "I'll talk to you some other time."

"Wait."

Halfway to the door, she paused. He rose and came around his desk. His fingers closed over her arm. "That was a cheap shot. I owe you an apology."

Tonya swallowed. "Accepted."

"Let me take you to lunch."

Uncertain, she raised her eyes to his. "I...I brought a sandwich."

"Leave it for tomorrow." His fingers still circled her arm, but his hold had softened to a gentle touch. He smiled, that stunningly wicked smile that set Tonya's pulse to pounding. "There's a little hole-in-the-wall a couple of blocks from here that serves the best tamales you ever ate."

"I love tamales."

"Let's go." As they walked down the hall, Kirk said, "You'll have to drive."

"You don't have a car?"

"Not with me. We just passed my transportation."

She stopped and looked back. "That motorcycle?"

He nodded and watched in surprise as she stopped and circled the black Harley parked in the hallway, then reached out to run her fingers over the handlebars. "It looks...sinister."

"It is."

"Why can't we take it?" she asked.

"You don't want to ride a motorcycle."

"Sure I do." She grinned at him. "I have a taste for danger."

So did he, evidently, since he'd asked her to lunch.

"Okay, I have a spare helmet in my office." He strode down the hall and returned a few minutes later. "It'll be too big for you."

"I'll manage." She tucked it under her arm and opened the door for him.

He guided the motorcycle across the yard, got on and waited for her to take her seat behind him. "Hold on." Her arms went around his waist and he took off.

As they careened around the corner, Kirk reflected that the danger to him didn't come from riding a motorcycle; what was risky was riding it with Tonya. Their proximity brought her scent to his nostrils. Her breasts pressed against his back. She was far too close. And he wanted her closer.

He pulled up before Mi Casita and wondered why he'd invited Tonya here. It wasn't one of those crowded, noisy Tex-Mex eateries that were so popular with the yuppies. She'd probably never been to a joint like this, he thought as he pushed open the door and the smell of chili surrounded them. This place was small and dark with a few booths and tables. Cracked vinyl covered the chairs and a small counter with a mirror behind it was adorned with neon signs advertising Mexican beers. A cooler in one corner held soft drinks. An old-fashioned radio behind the counter blasted out music from a Spanish station. The majority of customers were Hispanics, their conversations in their native tongue.

He steered Tonya to an empty booth and handed her a menu, a single typewritten sheet encased in plastic. "The place is clean," he mumbled in apology.

"I'm sure it is, and it smells wonderful. I'll have the tamales," she said, turning to the waitress, who had appeared at the table, "and iced tea."

Relieved at her easy acceptance of the restaurant, Kirk asked for a double order of tamales and a cola.

Within minutes, the hot, fragrant tamales were on the table. Tonya unwrapped the corn husk that enclosed the meat and tasted. "Mmm, you were right. These are the best." She took another bite and smiled. "Sam would love this place. Are they open on Saturday?"

Who was Sam? he wondered. Her lover, probably. A wave of jealousy burned in his gut. He should have realized she'd be involved with someone. "Yeah, they're open," he said through his teeth.

Tonya started on her second tamale. "I'll have to bring her then."

"Who?"

"Sam. She's my cousin."

"*She?*" Relief swept through him when Tonya nodded.

"Her name's Samantha. She's a private detective, if you can believe it, in business with her husband. They met working on a case for my grandfather."

"Interesting."

Tonya chattered on, bouncing from one topic to another—her family, a trip she'd taken, the kitten she'd adopted—and he listened, captivated. For a few moments, he forgot that they were from two different worlds, that she held the future of the OK Center in her hands, and he simply enjoyed the company of a beautiful, vivacious woman.

Reluctantly, he glanced at his watch. "I have a meeting with the captain of the local police substation in half an hour. We'd better go."

Tonya nodded. "This was wonderful. Thank you."

The sparkle in her eyes was thanks enough, Kirk thought as he paid the check and opened the door for her.

When they reached the Harley, he glanced across the street, then quickly turned back. "Damn!"

"What's wrong?" Tonya asked.

"Those kids over there, loitering by that building—no, don't turn around—they're members of the Sabers."

"A gang?" Tonya whispered, looking over at the group.

"Yeah, one of the toughest. They're involved in a turf war with Los Hermanos, a Hispanic gang. I wouldn't be surprised if they were planning a hit right now." He motioned to the cycle. "Let's go."

Back at the OK Center, Tonya got off the bike and paused a moment. "Are you going to tell the police about those gang members?"

"I'll mention it when I'm at the station, for as much good as it'll do," he answered. "They're not my main concern, though. Did you see the kid with them?"

"The tall, skinny one? Looked like he was eleven or twelve? Yes," she said.

"That's Toby Carson. He's got so much going for him, but he's starting to hang around with the wrong crowd. If we don't make some serious headway with him in the next few months, the Sabers will have him. They've already got him skipping school and running errands for them. Damn, there has to be a way to reach him." His muscles tensed with the habitual feeling of futility.

Tonya must have sensed his frustration because she put her hand on his arm as if to soothe him. For a moment, he let himself absorb the unfamiliar sensation of being cared for. But he resisted it and issued a stern warning to himself: *Don't get soft, Butler.* He couldn't afford to start leaning on someone, especially someone who'd be out of here before long.

As he started to push off on the motorcycle, she asked, "What's your meeting with the police about?"

Kirk shrugged. "Another useless attempt to get the cops involved in our programs."

"Mmm. See you later."

As he drove away, he noticed that she stood staring into space, her brows furrowed as if she was deep in thought. He wondered what was going on in that pretty head of hers. Had he said something wrong at lunch? The mention of gangs? His inability to get police participation? For a moment, he wondered how firm the Brewsters' commitment to this project was. And he realized how much power Tonya Brewster held over him.

TONYA SAT ON THE BENCH outside the fence and drew her jacket around her as she watched the kids assembled for basketball practice. The wind had picked up and the sky had clouded over. She could smell rain in the air.

On the other side of the fence eight youngsters stood in a little knot, engaging in what Tonya supposed was street talk, because it was incomprehensible to her. She was surprised to see that one of the youngsters was Toby Carson, the boy she and Kirk had seen earlier with members of the Sabers gang.

"Yo, Mr. Butler," Toby called, and Kirk came onto the court.

All Tonya could think was, *My God.* Dressed in gym shorts and a tank top, he was a woman's fantasy come alive. Broad shoulders, a glimpse of dark, curly chest hair, muscular thighs. Tonya felt herself melt despite the chill in the air. This center didn't need a grant from a foundation; they could make millions with a Kirk Butler calendar.

She noticed he wore an elastic bandage on his left leg and that the leg was scarred around the knee. She wondered if he'd been in a motorcycle accident.

Her eyes stayed riveted on him as practice got under way. He obviously knew what he was doing, pointing out weaknesses but also telling the kids how to correct them, and even a less-than-enthusiastic basketball fan like Tonya could see how good he was with the boys. He didn't allow for any nonsense on the court, but he encouraged each player with a phrase or a thumbs-up. The boys ate it up.

She was aware that Kirk spent extra time with Toby Carson, demonstrating a tricky move, praising the boy when he accomplished it.

Practice had been going on for about half an hour when another kid, a youngster of about twelve or thirteen, dashed across the grounds and onto the court. "Coach, I'm here," he panted.

Play stopped, the boys freezing like statues in a sports tableau. Slowly, Kirk turned and eyed the young man. "You're thirty minutes late." His voice was as chilly as the wind that now whipped his dark hair.

The youngster hung his head. "I...I know. Time...time jus' got away from me."

"You know the rules. Practice starts at four. Sit out the rest of the day."

Tonya had to strain to hear the boy's response. "Maybe I'll jus' go along home."

Kirk gave him a level look. "Up to you. You want to stay on the team, you sit and watch. You want off the team, then leave."

The boy shuffled over and sat on the bench outside the court. Kirk divided the players into two teams of four and began a practice game. The latecomer watched. Tonya watched him.

He had the build of a basketball player, tall and lanky with arms and legs that appeared too long for the rest of him. His skin was the color of light chocolate, and his short cropped hair shone midnight black. He sat still, head hanging, but after a few minutes he began to follow the game, muttering directives to the players, pantomiming their movements. Unaware of Tonya, he coached and played a one-man basketball game on the sidelines.

Tonya was entranced. Little by little, she scooted along the bench until she sat beside him. "You really like basketball, huh?" she said.

Startled, the boy turned to stare at her. "Where'd you come from?"

She chuckled. "I've been sitting here since practice started."

"I didn't see you."

"I know." Impulsively, she asked, "Why were you late?"

The smile disappeared and a glum expression took its place. "I dunno. I'm always late. I got to lookin' in a store window on the way home and then I remembered I forgot my practice shoes and I had to go back and the side door at school was locked so I had to go around and I remembered I had to talk to the math teacher and..."

Tonya smiled as he shrugged and turned back to the game. She felt a kindred spirit. "What's your name?"

"Huh? Oh, Germain Parker." Tonya introduced herself, and the boy suddenly turned and frowned at her. "Whatcha doin' here?" he asked. "You a caseworker or something? You one o' those juvenile probation officers?"

Tonya shook her head. "I'm just working here for a while."

He seemed to relax and turned back to the game. But only for a short time. "Watch this," he said to Tonya, and jumped up to execute a graceful leap and an imaginary hook shot. He grinned at her as his feet touched the ground. "I seen a ballet on TV once. Basketball's just like that, isn't it?"

Impressed by the comparison, Tonya nodded.

Apparently pleased by her acknowledgment, he demonstrated an imaginary dribble. "Great, huh?"

"I'd like to see you do it with a real ball."

He snickered, continuing his rhythmic demonstration. "You come out next game, an' you will...if I keep my grades up."

"Are you having trouble in school?" she asked.

"Nah. School's easy. But I los' my paper I was s'posed to turn in and if I don't find it, pow!" He demonstrated a punch to the midsection.

"Parker!" Kirk's voice cut into the conversation. "Are you watching this practice or not?"

"I'm watching," the boy grumbled. "I'm watching."

By the time the game ended, the sun was setting. Tonya and Germain watched Kirk lead the losing team in a cheer for the winners. "Practice day after tomorrow," Kirk said.

As the rest of the boys drifted away, Toby Carson hung back. "Coach, that move you showed me—it's Hakeem's, isn't it?"

Kirk nodded and dropped a hand on Toby's shoulder. "Sure is."

"If I work at it," the boy said earnestly, "I can make it mine, too."

"Come by tomorrow afternoon. We'll practice it again."

"Tomorrow's not a practice day."

"No problem."

The youngster's eyes lit up. "Thanks, Coach," he said, and bounded off.

Tossing the basketball from hand to hand, Kirk ambled over to the bench. "Show up late one more time, Germain, and you're off the team, understand?" In contrast to his tone with Toby, Kirk's voice was icy.

"Yeah, yeah," Germain muttered. Head down, he shuffled away. "How many Hakeem Olajuwons are there, anyway?" Tonya heard him say.

"You were pretty rough on him, weren't you?" she ventured as she and Kirk headed back inside.

"And *you* distracted him when he should have been watching practice."

Tonya bristled at the tone of his voice. Kirk the Curt, she thought. She tossed her head. "He didn't need me for that. If I hadn't been there, he'd have distracted himself."

"You an expert on that?" Kirk opened the door, then let it slam behind them. The hallway was dim, quiet. "How much do you know about kids, Ms. Brewster?" He put his hand on the wall and blocked her path.

"Not much, I admit, but—"

"You're here to oversee, not to interfere."

Furious now, Tonya gritted her teeth. She wished she had Sam's regal presence, but since she didn't, she'd make do with temper. "Let me pass." With both hands, she shoved against his chest. She might as well have tried to budge a steel beam. "You heard me," she demanded. "Let me by."

He moved his hand but not to allow her passage. Instead, it dropped to her shoulder. "Not just yet," he murmured, and bent his head.

Startled, Tonya moved to jerk away, but his mouth touched hers and she was trapped. Caught in a passion so hot and sweet she could hardly bear it. Effortlessly, his lips took possession of hers. Boldly, his tongue invaded her mouth.

She should stop this, but she couldn't. In an instant she was pressed against him, heart to heart, her hands fisted in his hair, her mouth taking even as it gave.

The kiss stole her breath, emptied her mind. She'd go anywhere with him, do anything. She tried to tell him but couldn't find her voice, could only cling to him. In the silent hallway, she could only listen to the sound of her heart beating painfully, and his thudding against her.

"Tonya," he whispered against her mouth. "Tonya, I—"

A scream shattered the stillness and cut off whatever he was about to say.

4

KIRK TURNED AND DASHED down the hall. Without hesitation, Tonya raced after him. He halted outside of the classroom where childbirth classes were held. Tonya skidded into him and he grabbed her shoulders. "Get back," he growled.

"But—"

"You heard me. Stay out of the way."

Another scream, long and terrified, sounded from the other side of the door. He didn't have to tell her again. Tonya shrank against the wall and held her breath as Kirk eased the door open. She didn't think she wanted to see what was happening inside the room, but she couldn't help looking.

"Rick Henderson," Kirk muttered, "and Janene North."

In the middle of the room stood a shaggy-haired youth, one arm thrown across the chest of a blond, pregnant girl, the other holding a gleaming knife to her throat. He was ugly. Blue eyes darting wildly around the room, teeth clenched, mouth twisted in a mock grin. A ragged scar distorted one pale cheek and made him look even more menacing. "Get outa here," he snarled as Kirk took a step into the room, "or I'll cut her." He edged the blade closer to the terrified girl's throat.

"No," she whispered. "No."

The police! She had to call them, Tonya thought. The

closest phone was in her office. She swung around, but a voice stopped her cold.

"Hey, you out there. Don't you go nowhere. Don't you get no ideas about callin' the cops, not unless you wanna see Janene here sliced up in little pieces."

Tonya nodded. "Okay." She stood still, pressed against the wall, needing its solidity to keep her upright. She'd never encountered violence before, never expected to. Cold sweat poured down her back. Her heart pounded so loudly she was certain the young hood could hear it.

"Come on, Rick." Kirk moved toward the boy and held out a hand. "Give me the knife. If you hurt her, you'll end up back in detention." His voice was low and calm.

Tonya let out a breath. Would Rick listen?

"Think I give a shit?" the youth sneered. "I'm gonna give her what she deserves." He gave the girl a shake. "You tell him," he growled at her. "Tell him to get outa the way."

"Please, Mr. Butler," the girl choked. "You heard what he said."

Tonya felt sick. What was she doing here? This was the stuff of TV cop shows, not her life. She should get out of here, sneak away when Rick wasn't looking, scurry back home where she belonged and never come back. But she couldn't move. Her eyes were riveted on the scene before her—on the waxen face of the young girl, on her staring blue eyes, the pupils dilated with shock. One sleeve of the girl's oversized T-shirt was torn. She had thrown one arm protectively over her protruding belly; the other flailed uselessly in the air.

Farther back in the room, Tonya saw a dozen other young faces, all of them terrified. Ladonna and a staff member named Corelle hunched in a corner, their arms sheltering several of the younger girls while they stared futilely at the couple before them.

Tonya's gaze shifted to Kirk. He'd taken a few steps back, but he didn't seem intimidated. He stood just inside the door, feet planted apart, arms at his sides, ready to move. "Let her go, Rick," he said.

Rick sneered. "I might, but I'm gonna hurt her a little first." He tightened his arm across the girl's breasts, and a snake tattooed on his bulging biceps seemed to slither toward his elbow. Janene let out a gasp as he yanked her closer.

Across the room, another pregnant girl began to sob. "I can't stand it. I want out of here. I wanna go home." She stumbled forward.

Rick's head snapped around. "Stay put, bitch," he ordered, and the girl scuttled back to the corner.

Ladonna pulled the frightened teenager into her arms. "Stay still, honey. You'll be all right," she cajoled, stroking the girl's hair.

While Rick's attention focused on Ladonna, Kirk edged closer.

Rick's head swiveled back. He fixed his gaze on Kirk. A string of obscenities poured from his mouth.

Unfazed, Kirk took another step toward him, then another.

The tip of the knife pricked the skin of Janene's neck. She shrieked.

"Shut up," Rick snarled.

Janene tightened her lips and whimpered softly. A thin ribbon of blood dripped onto her shirt.

As Kirk advanced toward them, Rick gave her another vicious jerk. "Okay, bitch, we're outa here."

"Please," the girl begged, but he dragged her toward the door. Halfway there, her knees buckled and she slid toward the floor. As Rick struggled with her limp body, Kirk lunged forward and grabbed the young thug's arm.

Metal flashed. Janene scrambled up and out of the way as Kirk and Rick grappled for the knife. The point grazed Kirk's arm.

"No," Tonya moaned. "No." She wanted to close her eyes, shut out the horrible scene the way she did in scary movies, but she couldn't. She kept watching.

Ladonna pulled Janene into the corner and hovered over her, trying to calm her.

Kirk caught Rick's wrist and forced it back, but only for a moment. The two fought for the knife. Grunting. Panting. Shoving. Neither able to budge the other.

The veins on Kirk's neck stood out, his lips curled in a grimace. He was strong, but Rick had the advantage of youth...and rage. Slowly, gradually, his hand inched forward, pushing Kirk's back.

Suddenly Kirk's arm went slack. Rick lost his balance and toppled forward. When Kirk grabbed him, the knife sailed across the room and landed with a harmless thunk.

"Thank God," Tonya muttered, but the words had barely left her lips when Rick's fist shot out and connected with Kirk's jaw. Kirk staggered backward, and the youth turned and bolted from the room. Kirk straightened and followed. "Call the cops," he yelled.

Tonya stood frozen against the wall as Rick, then Kirk raced past, close enough for her to feel their body heat. They disappeared down the hall, the sound of heavy footsteps echoing through the building. In a moment, the outside door slammed twice, and the hallway was silent.

Cautiously, Tonya started down the hall, peering into classrooms and offices as she went. What if Rick hadn't gone out at all? What if he was hiding in one of the rooms, waiting for someone to pass by? Nonsense. She'd heard the door slam twice. He had to be outside.

She slipped into her office and made the call, surprised

her voice was steady, then returned to the classroom. A babble of voices met her ears. Sobs, whimpers, questions. When she reached the door, she saw that Ladonna and Corelle were doing their best to calm the still-frightened youngsters. Tonya went to help.

Kirk had returned. Tonya paused where he knelt on the floor beside Janene. "Is Rick...?"

"Couldn't catch him," Kirk said. "Did you call?"

She nodded and looked down at Janene. The girl huddled on the floor. Her thin arms curved around her stomach, shielding the baby she carried. Her eyes were glazed, her mouth slack. Damp, blond hair half curtained the ashen skin of her face.

Kirk bent over Janene, stroked her hair. "You're okay," he soothed. "You don't have to be afraid anymore."

Janene sniffled. "H-he hurt me."

"We're gonna fix you up." Without turning, he said, "First aid kit's in the cabinet."

Tonya got it, put it on the floor beside him. He was still talking to Janene in that same calm voice. "Let's have a look." Tonya peered over his shoulder as he checked the girl's neck. "Just a scratch. I'm gonna put some antiseptic on it, and after the police talk to you, I'll take you home, okay?"

Janene whimpered as he cleansed the wound. "I don't wanna talk to no cops," she mumbled. Kirk continued to reassure her.

Tonya slipped past them. Kirk didn't need her help, but others did.

A small girl barely into her teens but well along in pregnancy sat rocking back and forth on the floor in a corner of the room. An older girl had gotten sick all over her bright blue jacket. Several were crying, others gazed fearfully out the windows.

Ladonna and Corelle tended as many as they could. Tonya joined in. Helping the girls calmed her own fears, lessened her horror at what she'd seen.

She saw Kirk shut the first aid kit and sit back on his heels. "Can you tell me what happened?" he said to Janene.

She took a hiccuping breath. "Before Rick went to detention, I was his woman."

Woman? Tonya thought, looking at the bony girl. Janene was barely past childhood. On the other hand, she was physically mature enough for sex. And its consequences.

"He thinks I cheated on him."

"Thinks the baby isn't his?" Kirk asked.

"Yes, but it is, Mr. Butler. I told him and told him..." Her words dissolved in a torrent of tears. Patiently, Kirk sat beside her, soothing her.

Suddenly, the noise in the room subsided. Every head turned toward the door. Tonya looked over her shoulder and saw two uniformed police officers in the doorway. Kirk rose and walked over to them. They spoke in low tones for a few minutes, then Kirk led them to Janene.

The female officer, a tall sandy-haired woman, knelt beside the girl. "We want to ask you a few questions, okay?"

Janene nodded. "Yes, ma'am."

"What happened a while ago?"

She repeated her story.

"Any idea where Rick might've gone?"

"No, ma'am. He stays different places. He doesn't tell where."

"How about some of his friends? Can you tell me where they live?"

Janene's face paled. "Oh, no, ma'am, I couldn't do that. I...I don't really know."

Tonya could see she was lying, but she couldn't say she blamed the girl. If Rick's friends were anything like him, she doubted Janene would want to get on their bad side. Giving their addresses to the police would be a sure way to make them mad.

The policewoman sighed and glanced up at her partner. A look that spoke volumes passed between them. She rose and spoke to Kirk. "We'll do our best to locate him. You going to file charges?"

"You bet we are."

She nodded. "We'll be in touch."

When the two officers left, Kirk turned to Ladonna. "Give me your keys." She reached in her pocket and handed them to him, and he helped Janene up. "I'm taking Janene home," he said. "The rest of you stay here. Don't anyone leave until I get back."

"Why?"

"Why can't we go home?"

"I'll tell you why," a tall African American girl answered. "'Cause Rick gonna be out front with the Sabers."

Someone began to wail. "No-o."

"Shut your mouth, girl," another teenager ordered. "What you know about the Sabers anyhow? You jus' a dumb bitch."

"Who you callin' a dumb bitch?"

Within seconds the two were on the floor, pinching, punching, pulling hair. Bedlam erupted as girls took sides, spurring the two fighters on. Others began to cry. The girl Tonya had succeeded in calming now cowered in the corner again, covering her ears.

"Stop it!" Ladonna's voice rang out with the authority of a drill sergeant. The girls, even the pair on the floor, froze. "All right, last thing we need in here is more violence. Get up, you two, and don't let me see either one of you lift your little finger, hear?"

The sullen combatants stalked to opposite sides of the

room. The others gathered in groups, chattering about Rick and Janene while they waited for Kirk. At least no one was crying.

Tonya walked over to Ladonna, who leaned against the wall. "The Sabers are a gang, aren't they?"

Ladonna sighed. "The worst. Rick is one of the big guns and that ain't no pun. The Sabers are armed to the teeth. We were lucky he didn't have his gun with him today."

Tonya shivered. Instead of going home, she should drive to her grandfather's and hand in her resignation. Even *he* couldn't fault her if she refused to come back here. She should return to her original plan of setting up mystery weekends for the Whodunit bookstore. Imaginary murders, not the real thing. Weekend fun, not gang warfare.

Kirk walked into the room.

His knowing eyes met hers. *He thinks I'm going to bail out.* And she should.

In the face of the challenge in his eyes, all the *shoulds* disappeared. Damned if she'd quit. If the rest of them could take it, so could she. She'd be back tomorrow *and* the day after that. She'd stick it out for the whole six months.

LATER THAT NIGHT Tonya sat in her living room, the kitten curled in her lap, a cup of hot chocolate on the table beside her. On the stereo, a Chopin prelude played softly. She'd turned the lamp low.

A quiet scene. The earlier events of the day were far away in another world, but they refused to disappear. No matter how hard she tried to concentrate on the music, the steaming chocolate and the comforting sound of the cat's purr, she couldn't stop thinking about the last few hours. The basketball practice, her conversation with Germain Parker, Janene's piercing screams and the ugly scene with

Rick. Everything that had happened raced through her mind like a video on fast forward.

Then it rewound, pausing in a freeze-frame, zooming in on Kirk's kiss. The power of it, the excitement. Those few minutes in his arms were etched indelibly in her mind. Even thinking about that kiss, she felt her pulse begin to pound.

Who was he? She'd seen so many sides of him today: the tough, streetwise guy who'd wrested a knife from a violent kid; the compassionate man who'd comforted Janene; the lover whose potent kiss had overwhelmed her.

What next? That he wanted her was clear from the way he'd held and kissed her, but he wasn't the first man who had. She'd said no more times than she'd said yes.

He was different from most of the men she'd known. Her grandfather would say he was rough around the edges. Not so different from Clint himself, Tonya mused.

She wished she and Kirk had had a chance to talk, but when he walked her to her truck, she was only one of a crowd. He'd grasped her arm impersonally as if she were a stranger. When she'd climbed into the truck, he'd said nothing but "Lock the doors." She would have appreciated a word of comfort, the kind of reassurance she'd heard him give Corelle and Ladonna and their teenage charges when he helped them herd the girls into their cars to drive them home.

Tonya leaned back and shut her eyes. God, Kirk Butler was perplexing. She was too tired to try to figure him out now. Maybe tomorrow.

NOT BOTHERING to shut the door, Kirk strode into his office the next morning. He ignored his chair and remained standing, staring out the window. Wearily, he massaged his neck. He hadn't gotten much sleep last night, and his body made a point of reminding him. Especially his knee.

He'd have to talk to Rick's parole officer. That kid posed a real threat to the neighborhood. Under his leadership the Sabers had thrived. They'd become the toughest, most feared gang in the area, and now that Rick was on the streets again, they could only get worse.

Toby Carson was Rick's cousin. That meant he was almost a lost cause. "No, damn it," Kirk muttered. He wouldn't let that happen. He'd continue to use basketball as a vehicle to win Toby's trust. He'd—

Behind him, he heard light footsteps. Who'd be here this early? He swung around and came face-to-face with Tonya. For a moment, he only stared, wondering if he'd fallen asleep and dreamed her.

Before he could speak, she stepped closer. "Your jaw," she murmured. "It's bruised where Rick hit you." Gingerly, she touched him, her fingertips barely grazing his skin.

He jerked back as if she'd burned him. "I'm fine." Half-dazed, he stared at her. She was so beautiful, so... "What are you doing here?" he snapped. "I thought you'd be at home in your cozy little apartment, as far away as you could get."

She flinched as if she'd been slapped. "I'm back," she said, and he thought he saw tears glitter in her eyes. "And I'll keep coming back. Regardless of what you think."

He didn't know what he thought...or what he felt. Desire, resentment at her position here, grudging respect that she'd shown up in spite of what happened. And, mostly, confusion. He didn't like being confused and he was angry at her for making him feel that way. "You're a fool for coming back," he growled.

Her eyes narrowed, and he saw again the determination

he'd only glimpsed when they'd first met. "No, *you* are," she said, her voice stronger than he expected. "If you thought that little disturbance last night would keep me away, think again."

Rage at her naïveté and her stubbornness made him lash out again. "That 'little disturbance' should have sent you a message loud and clear. I told you before, you don't belong here."

She raised her chin, then turned her back on him and walked out of the office. "We'll see," she said over her shoulder, and slammed the door in his face.

5

KIRK DROPPED into his chair, put his elbows on the desk and rested his head on his hands. Damn, he'd made a mess of things. He'd just called the woman who held the purse strings for the OK Center a fool. Nonprofit or not, the center was a business, and this was no way to run a business.

Who was he kidding? What had happened between him and Tonya just now had had nothing to do with business. It was personal. Extremely personal.

When her fingers had whispered across his jaw, the shock of that featherlight contact had leapt through him with the force of a speeding Harley. The sharp rush of desire had been so strong it was painful. Thank God, Tonya's eyes had been on his face. If she'd looked down, she'd have seen the evidence—the hard evidence—of that desire.

He'd wanted to hold her again, explore her mouth, strip off her clothes and make love to her—right here on his desk. Just thinking about it aroused him all over again.

Why the hell had she come back? She didn't belong in a neighborhood like this, where young punks held knives to the throats of girls they were supposed to be in love with. She belonged in some rich enclave where knives were used to carve chateaubriand, not people. Above all, she belonged somewhere safe.

Despite her determination to stay, sooner or later she'd figure it out. Then she'd walk away from here without a backward glance. That was why he'd struck out at her. Self-protection, pure and simple.

In the meantime, he'd do what he'd intended from the first: avoid her.

BY AFTERNOON TONYA WAS still fuming. Kirk had not only infuriated her, he'd hurt her, and she wouldn't forgive him easily.

Oh, heck. Yes, she probably would. She rarely held a grudge longer than a day.

Okay, she'd forgive what he'd said, but she wouldn't forget. And she'd prove to him she was made of stronger stuff than he thought.

Now, though, she had a meeting scheduled. Ladonna was next on her list.

Tonya was careful to take notes during their session. If not, she was sure she'd forget everything Ladonna said because her run-in with Kirk had distracted her.

After she and Ladonna had finished their discussion, she was tempted to quiz the woman about Kirk. Maybe if she knew more about him, she'd understand his quicksilver mood changes.

But Ladonna rose and reached for her jacket. "I'm gonna take a walk over to Janene's house and see how she's getting along."

"I'll go with you," Tonya said. She hurried back to her office to get her coat and joined Ladonna at the door.

As they strolled down the street, they passed students on the way home from school. Three giggling girls in bright red jackets sashayed by, their gait designed to attract the attention of every teenage boy around. One girl's jacket barely covered her jutting belly.

"So many of these kids are pregnant," Tonya said. "You must've had at least a dozen at the Center yesterday, and...there's another." She nodded toward a girl in a blue jacket who looked ready to deliver...and who couldn't have been more than thirteen years old.

"You better believe it, girlfriend," Ladonna said. "These little sisters give birth like rabbits." She laughed when Tonya shook her head in disbelief. "You never saw anything like it, did you?"

"No. Life must be tough for them, becoming mothers while they're still babies themselves."

"Darn right," Ladonna agreed. "I know."

Tonya turned to her in surprise. "You mean—"

"Yeah, I mean I was pregnant with Danisha, my first little girl, when I was thirteen. She was born 'bout a month after my fourteenth birthday. Simon was born the next year."

"How could you take care of them and still go to school?"

"I couldn't. I dropped out." She chuckled at Tonya's shocked expression. "Girl, droppin' out of school was no big deal. 'Bout everyone I knew was doin' the same thing."

Tonya digested this as they waited at the corner for a school bus to pass. Noisy laughter drifted through the windows, and a grinning teenage boy leaned out and whistled at them. "Didn't you tell me you knew Kirk after college?" she asked.

"Yeah," Ladonna said, "but that was later. Time I was sixteen, I was mostly high on crack—the dude I was livin' with got me hooked. Problem was, I was pregnant again." Her smile faded. "You ever seen a crack baby?"

Tonya shook her head.

"It's not a pretty sight. Fanetta was a mess, but you know what? I didn't care. I was so outa control, I didn't care nothin' for her or nobody, my older kids included. Then she died."

Tonya didn't know what to say. She reached for Ladonna's hand. For a moment, they were both silent. Tonya's eyes filled with tears. The girl who passed them on the sidewalk was a red blur.

"She was so little." Ladonna spoke in a faraway voice as if she could see her lost child. "Just three months old and nothin' but a mess of bones." She took a long breath. "When I buried that baby, I knew I had to change my life or me and my other babies would all be headin' straight to hell."

"And you did change."

"Yeah. First thing, I kicked that brother who got me on crack out of the house, then I went to drug rehab. Wasn't easy, but I quit using, got my GED and went to college on a special scholarship. And now here I am. I'm part of something good, helping other sisters have a better life than I did—keeping them away from drugs, teaching them about birth control, showing them they got something goin' for them besides goin' to bed with the first dude that walks by. Or if they're already pregnant, helping them learn how to take care of themselves and their babies.

"And the best thing is, I got two great kids. Wanna see?" She pulled out her wallet and pointed to two pictures. "Danisha's eighteen and Simon's almost seventeen."

"They're beautiful," Tonya said sincerely.

"Thanks. Here we are." She slowed as they came to a small gray house. Or, Tonya thought, maybe it used to be white and had faded. A redbud tree in the front yard was trying to bloom without much success. A scrawny yellow dog trotted across the yard and wagged his tail. Tonya stopped to pet the friendly mutt and, as she looked up, noticed the motorcycle in the driveway. It was the same model as—

"Is that Kirk's?"

"Sure looks like it," Ladonna said. "I guess he's checkin' on Janene, too."

Great! The last person Tonya wanted to see. She hadn't passed her twenty-four-hour limit on grudges. She was still hopping mad at him, and she wasn't very good at concealing her emotions. With a baleful look at the motorcycle, she followed Ladonna to the door. Ladonna knocked, and in a moment a thin woman with lank blond hair and tired eyes answered and invited them in. Ladonna introduced Tonya to Mary Lou North, Janene's mother.

Kirk wasn't in the living room.

Relieved, Tonya let out a breath and glanced around. The interior of the house looked as ill-kempt as the outside. Dust covered every surface, faded curtains sagged at the windows, one arm of the couch was marred by a cigarette burn. A pile of magazines lay on the floor in front of an armchair. A soap blared on the TV.

"Y'all come on in the kitchen," Mary Lou said. The smell of something cooking on the stove met them as they entered.

At the kitchen table sat Kirk, his commanding presence dominating the small room.

Their eyes met.

She wouldn't be daunted by that lethal stare. Tonya kept her eyes on his, her gaze never wavering. Around her, the room heated. Amazing how blistering a mere look could be.

Taking his time, Kirk rose to his feet. In another man, Tonya thought, that gesture might have been gentlemanly; in Kirk, it was arrogant. His gaze still locked with hers, he pulled out the chair next to him and indicated that she should sit.

She didn't want to take that chair, but Ladonna and Mrs.

North were already seated; it was the only place left. Tonya pulled the chair as far from Kirk as she could and sat.

"I'm surprised to see you here," he said to her in a low voice.

There he goes again. "Why?" she murmured so only he could hear. "I was there yesterday. I wanted to see how Janene is getting along." She turned to the girl's mother. "How is she?"

Mrs. North shrugged. "Okay. She's in her room. She was too scared to go to school today. She can't hide forever, though. They'll be sending one of those truant officers after her. Janene," she called, "come out here."

In a moment, the girl appeared. She stood in the doorway, barefoot, dressed in a man's long-sleeved shirt. Tonya looked at her tear-streaked face and realized that in a few years Janene would look like her mother—blank-faced and exhausted.

Kirk got up and went to Janene. Taking her arm, he drew her gently to his chair. "How are you feeling?" he asked.

"I'm okay," she said, staring at the floor.

"Janene," Mrs. North said, "you go get Mr. Butler another chair outa the living room."

"I'll get it," Kirk said.

"No, sir. Janene will do it. She needs to make herself useful around here 'stead of just sittin' around mooning over that punk Rick."

Janene gave her mother a sullen look but went to get the chair. She dragged it to Tonya's side. Kirk sat down. Now he was practically in Tonya's lap. She gave him a sidelong glance and found his eyes on her. Quickly, she faced front again and tried unobtrusively to move as far from Kirk as she could without falling off the chair. Beside her, he shifted. His leg brushed hers and both she and Kirk jolted.

Forget he's there. Easy to say but not so simple to do when he sat so close she could sense his every breath. Annoyed and uncomfortable, she made an effort to concentrate on the conversation.

"I won't be comin' back to the center for those childbirth classes," Janene said to Ladonna. "Rick doesn't want me goin' over there."

"Honey," Ladonna said, "you have to come back to the class. You need to know what to expect during pregnancy and how to take care of yourself. And if you're going to keep this baby, you have to learn how to care for it."

"Well, I don't know if I'm gonna keep it. And Rick said—"

"Rick!" Mrs. North cried, grasping the edge of the table as if she might shove it over. "I told Janene if she got mixed up with that lowlife she'd be sorry for it." Her voice rose and she pointed a bony finger at her daughter. "But did she listen? No, she had to go and get herself in trouble. Now she's got a kid comin' and Rick after her, and..." Mary Lou North began to cry. "I don't know what we're gonna do. Every night I go to bed scared to death. I hear those cars drivin' past, and one night I know someone's gonna shoot at us. We've been sleepin' on the floor. I worry every day till Janene gets home from school, but what can I do? I can't keep her locked up in the house."

"Mary Lou." Ladonna handed the sobbing woman a tissue and put an arm around her shaking shoulders. "Of course, Janene has to go to school. Can you drive her?"

Mary Lou shook her head slowly. "I have to leave here at six to get to my aide job at the hospital. I work the seven to three shift."

"I can pick her up," Tonya offered.

"No," Kirk said.

She was about to insist, but beneath the table, he caught

her wrist. Hoping she was being unobtrusive, she tried to tug her arm away. Useless.

"Janene needs more than a ride—she needs protection," he said reasonably, and Tonya realized he was right. "I'll pick her up." He continued to hold on to Tonya as if he were a bulldog and her arm were a bone.

"Oh, we couldn't put you to that kinda trouble." Mary Lou seemed unaware of the byplay going on under the table.

"No problem." Kirk's voice was pleasant, calm. "I'll drive her to school and the Center and take her home until this dies down or the police pick up Rick." He turned to Janene and fixed the girl with a stern look. "Do you know where Rick is?"

"No."

"Janene North—" her mother began.

"Mama, I told you and *told* you, I don't know where he'd go." Her cheeks flushed and she shot her mother an angry look. "Why don't you ask one of the Sabers? They're the only ones who'd know."

"Don't you go sassin' me, young lady," her mother warned.

Ladonna put an end to the argument by rising. "We need to get going. Mary Lou, if we can help you out with anything, you call. Janene, I'll see you in class tomorrow."

Kirk and Tonya got up, too. He dropped her arm. Shooting him a pointed look, she rubbed it.

"I sure do thank you," Mary Lou said, following them to the door.

As soon as it shut behind them, Kirk took Tonya's arm again. "Let me go," she muttered.

"After we talk." He turned to Ladonna. "We'll be right back." He started across the yard, keeping Tonya firmly in tow.

"You don't have to hold on to me," she snapped. "I'm not going to run away."

"Now, why don't I believe you?" He let go of her wrist but took her elbow in a firm grasp and led her to his motorcycle.

"What?" Tonya raised her chin.

"Did you have any idea how dangerous it would be for you to pick up Janene?" he asked, his voice low and furious.

"I didn't think about it," she admitted, then took the offensive. "How about you? Did you think how little protection she'd get on a motorcycle?"

His lips thinned. "Of course. I'm going to use Ramon's car." He came a step closer. Across the yard Ladonna stared at them, a puzzled frown on her face. "Now, back to you. What would your foundation say if something happened to you?"

That hurt. "Are you worried they'd cut off the grant?"

"No, damn it," he muttered, and she saw something flash in his eyes. Tenderness? Concern? It disappeared so quickly she couldn't tell. "I'm worried about you."

She wanted to ask him why, but she wasn't sure she'd like his answer. Instead, she shook him off. "Don't be. I can take care of myself."

"Great. Fine." With a snort of disgust, he mounted the motorcycle. As Tonya walked across the yard and joined Ladonna on the sidewalk, he sped away.

To Ladonna's credit, she made no comments and asked no questions as she and Tonya walked back to the OK Center.

SWEAT POURED DOWN Kirk's back and dripped from his face as he concentrated on the rowing machine. Beside him, Ramon's muscles bunched as he worked his triceps with hand weights.

The gym was the best place Kirk knew to unwind. A place to leave the worries of the day behind and concentrate on pure physical activity. He liked taxing his muscles to the maximum, liked the camaraderie of male conversation.

He didn't favor one of those fancy coed health clubs with piped-in music and state-of-the-art machines. The gym around the corner from his apartment was old and basic. A place for guys. It was open to both genders, of course, but few women frequented it, just a couple of female body-builders with bulging biceps.

This evening the patrons were all male, the conversation limited to three topics—business, sports and sex. Two guys down the way were discussing the upcoming baseball season as they pedaled side by side on stationary bicycles. On his other side, above the sound of treadmills, Kirk heard an argument about the stock market and a couple of dirty jokes.

When he had finished his usual workout, Kirk headed for the shower, then the sauna. He chose a bench and leaned back, enjoying the heat, the faint smell of cedar. He felt utterly relaxed.

Ramon followed him in and sat beside him. He let out a long sigh. "This is the life, *amigo*."

"Nothing like a good workout to relax you, especially the way our week's been going."

Ramon yawned. "Things will calm down."

"Yeah, when pigs fly."

"Come on, buddy, we haven't got it so bad. In fact, that grant's put us on easy street."

Kirk felt some of the tension return to his body. "I'd ap-

preciate the damn grant a lot more if it came without
strings.''

"So would I, but Tonya's not hard to deal with. She's settling in well.''

Kirk muttered an oath under his breath.

"You disagree?'' Ramon grinned. "I'd, uh, gotten the impression you kinda liked her.''

Kirk straightened. He was definitely feeling tense now.
"What gave you that idea?''

"The way you look at her.''

Kirk sighed and figured he might as well admit it. "Yeah,
but I'd like her better if she didn't hold our future in her
hands.''

"That's always the problem, isn't it?'' Ramon said, study-
ing Kirk with penetrating brown eyes. "You don't want a
woman to have the upper hand. You've got to be in control
in your relationships. No compromises.''

"Hey,'' Kirk said, not liking this conversation at all, "I
thought we were talking about the center, not my personal
life.''

"We were, but if you get personal with Tonya, it'll be the
same thing.'' Ramon sat up beside him. "Compromise.
That's the secret in personal relationships.''

"Your wife taught you that, huh?''

"Drummed it into my hard head. Damned good thing
she did. You gotta learn it, too, *amigo*, if you want your relationships to go anywhere.''

"Thanks for the tip, but I don't have a relationship with
Tonya Brewster.'' He chose to forget the way he'd kissed
her the other night, the way he'd wanted to kiss her this
morning. "I'm not looking for a long-term arrangement
with anyone,'' he said firmly.

"That's clear. As soon as a relationship gets serious, you
ease out of it. You're nice to them, you leave them happy,

but you still leave." Ramon hesitated a moment, then added, "You got burned once, but that was a long time ago."

"Once burned, twice shy."

"Crap," Ramon said. "And that's my last word on it."

"AND HE TOLD ME AGAIN I don't belong there," Tonya was saying to Sam as they strolled through the elegant Galleria Shopping Center on Saturday afternoon.

"Did you ask him why?"

"He keeps saying it's too dangerous."

Sam smiled. "That's what Wade used to tell me, too."

"Totally different situation *and* relationship," Tonya said. "Wade was crazy about you. From the start."

"So? Maybe Kirk Butler feels the same way about you."

"Impossible! He doesn't feel any way about me. He's just an...an infuriating, exasperating, arrogant a—"

"Watch your mouth, cuz." Sam grinned. "He's certainly gotten your attention if you've noticed all that about him. What else?"

"Well, he's the most confusing man I've ever met." Tonya sighed. "One minute he's chewing me out, the next minute he's kis—" Her cheeks flushed as her voice trailed off.

"Yes? You were saying?"

"Nothing."

"Sounded like 'kissing' to me."

"Well," Tonya mumbled, "he did kiss me once."

Sam laughed. "I rest my case." She paused in front of an athletics store. "Let's go in here. I need some warm-up pants."

Tonya followed her in but paid little attention to the displays of clothing. Could Sam be right? Could Kirk be crazy about her? Though the idea intrigued her, she doubted it.

She waited while Sam tried on the pants, then said, "If I can just convince Kirk that I fit in over there, part of the problem will be solved."

"He'll still be arrogant and exasperating," Sam pointed out.

"Yeah, but I won't mind so much."

While Sam paid for the pants, Tonya leaned against the counter and gazed abstractedly around the store. Her eyes lit on a rack of nylon jackets and she wandered over to inspect them. The weather was getting warmer, and she needed something lighter to wear.

"Ready?" Sam joined her.

"No, just a minute. I think I'll get one of these jackets. Everyone at the center wears these."

"One more way to fit in."

"Yep." Tonya rifled through the garments. "The color of choice for the staff seems to be gray." She wrinkled her nose.

"Obviously not your choice," Sam said. "Let me guess. Red."

Tonya nodded as she made her selection. "I've seen a lot of red ones. They're practically a neighborhood uniform. Be right back."

Smiling to herself, she draped the jacket over her arm and headed for the cash register. Most of the staff at the OK Center looked pretty drab. *She'd* liven up the place, add some color to the surroundings, maybe start a new trend. Who could argue with that? They'd probably even be pleased.

6

TONYA SLAMMED THE DOOR of the pickup and hurried across the yard of the OK Center. The wind was brisk this morning and it was starting to rain. She was glad she'd worn her new jacket. Inside the building she slowed her steps and called a cheerful good-morning to Corelle and one of the women on the day-care staff.

Both women halted. Neither said a word. They stood staring at her with open mouths. Probably surprised she'd arrived so early. Tonya shrugged and continued down the hall.

She put her briefcase on her desk and shivered. The heat didn't seem to be on. Or maybe it was too early for the building to have warmed up. "Coffee," she decided, and headed for the kitchen.

The aroma of fresh coffee and the sound of voices drifted down the hall. She heard Ladonna's throaty chuckle and Ramon's answering laugh. Good. She needed to talk to them about an idea that had been bouncing around in her head. "Good morning," she said as she entered the room.

Ladonna and Ramon looked up. "Good m—" Ladonna clapped a hand to her mouth. Her eyes widened.

So did Ramon's. "*Mamacita*," he whispered.

"Wh—" Tonya began.

"Holy hell!" The outraged voice came from behind her.

Tonya spun around. Kirk stood in the doorway, looking

big and furious. "What—" She tried again, but he didn't give her time to finish.

"Where in hell did you get that?"

She held up her hands to show him they were empty. "Get what?"

"That jacket," he snarled.

Confused, Tonya peered down at herself. Was the jacket too small? Was it torn? Stained? It seemed fine to her and exactly like all the others she'd noticed. "I've seen a million of them. What's wrong with it?"

"Wrong?" He took a step toward her, then, thankfully, stopped. He looked as if he'd explode at any moment. He shook his head and turned to Ramon. "Tell her."

"Tonya," Ramon said quietly. "Red is the Sabers' color. If you wear a jacket like that, it means..." His cheeks turned as crimson as the jacket. "Well, it says..."

"It means you're either a member of the Sabers or you're sleeping with one," Ladonna said.

"Oh." Tonya squeezed her eyes shut. "Oh, Lord. I thought it was a fad or the high school color or something." Horrified, she tugged at the zipper; it caught halfway down. Feeling like an idiot, she jerked it ineffectually.

"Here, let me," Ladonna said, and worked the zipper down the rest of the way.

Tonya pulled off the jacket. "Trash can," she muttered, and dumped it in. "I'll, uh, check with you next time before I go shopping," she said, forcing a smile. Trying for a reasonably dignified exit, she strode out of the kitchen. She didn't need coffee to warm her anymore. Her cheeks were flaming, and she felt hot all over.

In the hall she leaned against the wall and shut her eyes again. "Stupid, stupid, stupid," she muttered.

From the kitchen, the sound of Kirk's disgusted voice

carried easily. "Of all the stupid things to do." Well, at least she and Kirk agreed on something.

"Come on, *amigo*," Ramon said. "She made a natural mistake. Everyone wears those jackets. How could she know?"

"My point exactly. She *doesn't* know."

"She'll learn," Ramon replied. "And the last thing we need is conflict here. We have enough of that in the neighborhood."

"Yeah, right. But I don't want her to—"

Unable to listen to any more, Tonya scurried down the hall to the safety of her office. Once inside, she shut the door, sank onto her chair and dropped her head in her hands. Why did she always make a mess of things? She had a chronic case of foot-in-mouth disease. She started with such good intentions, then somewhere along the way, she made a mistake and botched up everything. The voice of her seventh-grade teacher echoed in her mind. "You're so impulsive, Tonya. You never think things through."

She wished she'd waited to hear Kirk finish what he'd started to say. "I don't want her to—" To what? Stay here? That was obvious.

What would her grandfather say about the jacket incident? If she told him—which she didn't intend to—he'd probably laugh. She could hear him now, his trademark belly laugh rumbling through the room. "Hell with it," he'd say. "Get on with your work."

But Clint Brewster had a lot more confidence in himself than Tonya had in herself. He also apparently had a lot more confidence in *her* than she did. He'd sent her here, hadn't he? Damn, she wished he hadn't. Selling clothes, such an easy, mindless job, sounded better and better. If only she hadn't quit. Then her grandfather would have left her alone.

"But," she muttered, sitting up straight, "you did quit your job and he did send you here, and, damn it, this time you're going to stick it out." In some way she sensed but didn't yet understand, "this time" was too important for her to walk out.

She opened her briefcase and pulled out her daily planner. Today she was to meet with Ramon. Thank goodness she'd already had her meeting with Kirk. She didn't think she could handle another confrontation with him this morning. She was glad Ramon was the center administrator, not Kirk. Ramon was a peacemaker.

Kirk, on the other hand, would just barrel over people and situations like a tank. He was more like her, Tonya thought. Bigger and more intimidating but possessed of the same tunnel vision. He, too, aimed straight for his goal without checking out alternative pathways or noticing the pitfalls along the way.

Shaking off thoughts of Kirk, Tonya searched for the list of questions she wanted to ask Ramon. She'd spent a long time on them and felt they were good ones. Most concerned the use of existing funds. She read them over again, then smoothed her hair and put on fresh lipstick. Pink, not red.

When she opened her door, she felt a moment of nerves. She glanced both ways down the hall, then sighed with relief. As long as she didn't run into Kirk and have to endure his hostile gaze, she'd be fine. And if she did— Well, one thing for certain. She wouldn't apologize. She'd made a mistake, she'd rectified it by getting rid of the jacket, and she wouldn't give Kirk the pleasure of seeing her grovel.

Luck remained with her. Ramon was alone when she went to his office. The door was open, and he glanced up and smiled as Tonya paused on the threshold. "Hi, come in."

She took a chair and laid the paper with her list of questions in front of her on the desk. The first question was—

"About this morning," Ramon said.

Here we go. Was he going to tell her to leave? Not likely. He couldn't unless he returned the grant, and she was certain he didn't intend to do that. Her first impulse was to mumble an apology. *Don't,* she ordered herself, and managed to thwart her natural instinct.

"I apologize..." he began.

Apologize? *Ramon* was apologizing?

"For Kirk," he said.

"Never mind. I'll speak for myself."

Tonya swung around and saw Kirk lounging in the doorway. Why did he always have to sneak up behind her? Her stomach dropped.

Ramon gave Kirk a pointed look as he sat down next to Tonya. The look wasn't lost on her. Ramon had probably invited Kirk to this meeting so they could all share their grievances. Fine. All she had to do was keep quiet. As long as she used her brain instead of her mouth, she could maintain the advantage.

She glanced at Kirk, but could read nothing in his dark eyes. She waited.

"I sounded angry this morning," he began.

"Sounded?" Tonya snorted. "You *were* angry."

He shook his head. "I was worried."

That hadn't crossed her mind. She stared at Kirk. "About what?"

"The center, for one thing. You may not realize it, but colors are a big thing around here. You wear the wrong color, even the wrong shade, you're begging for trouble. The Sabers are red. Los Hermanos are blue. I told you they're in a turf war. For someone here to wear Saber colors could escalate it, bring it right to our doorstep."

So that was why Ladonna, Corelle and the others wore neutral browns and grays. Not from a lack of fashion sense—for survival.

"This is real life," he added, "not 'West Side Story.' These guys don't sing and dance. They shoot."

His ominous tone made Tonya shiver. She cleared her throat. "You said 'for one thing.' What else are you worried about?"

"You."

Worried about her? This was the second time he'd said that. Wide-eyed, she stared at him. Her mouth opened but nothing came out.

"In that jacket, you were a walking target. If one of the Hermanos had seen you, he wouldn't have thought twice about blowing your head off."

She shuddered again. Automatically, she hugged herself.

"There are a couple of other gangs around here, too," Kirk said, rising and looming over her. "Learn their colors. Don't put yourself—or the center—in this situation again. This is neutral territory. We need to keep it that way."

He started for the door, then paused. "This morning was a close call. Don't give us another." With that, he left Tonya and Ramon to their meeting.

THE FOLLOWING DAY Kirk sat sprawled in his chair as the staff meeting got under way. He glanced thoughtfully at Tonya. God, she was something. He'd almost exploded when he'd seen her wearing that Saber red jacket yesterday morning. He couldn't bear thinking about it. She'd thought he was angry at her. What she didn't realize was that he'd been terrified, thinking what could have happened to her. A picture had flashed in his mind—Tonya lying in a heap in front of the center, her chest pierced by a bullet, blood pouring out. Just as well she couldn't read his thoughts, had no idea how much time he spent worrying about her. Their relationship was already getting complicated enough. Let her think he was just angry, since he was that, too.

Ramon, the voice of reason as usual, was right. Tonya didn't know about gang wars. But, damn it, if she was going to park herself here, she should have made it her business to find out. They were lucky nothing had happened.

He toyed with the silver buckle at his waist. The incident was over. Why was it still bugging him? *Easy answer, Butler. Everything about the lady bugs you.* Disgusted with himself, he scowled. Tonya glanced at him, then quickly looked away. Probably thought he was still mad. He was, but at himself.

"Okay, *compadres*, we have a lot to go over today." Ramon began the meeting. "Let's start with Rick Henderson. Anyone know if he's surfaced?"

The others shook their heads. "Janene may, but she's not talking," Kirk said.

"Scared?"

"Either that or she's keeping quiet because of a misplaced sense of loyalty." Frustrated, he raked his fingers through his hair. "Rick could be anywhere, and he could turn up again any time."

Tonya stared at him, her eyes wide. "Aren't the police still looking for him?"

"Sure," Kirk said, "but whether they'll find him is anybody's guess. His cohorts aren't talking. Hell, they're probably hiding him. And face it, the cops have got other things to do. Rick Henderson's whereabouts aren't at the top of their priority list. So—" he leaned forward and lowered his voice to a growl "—keep that in mind and don't go wandering around the neighborhood."

Tonya swallowed and nodded. But would she really listen, Kirk wondered. He'd told her not to come out here in the first place, and she hadn't paid attention to his advice. Headstrong woman. He'd like to take her by the shoulders and shake some sense into her. He'd like to...

To pull her into his arms and finish what he'd started the other night. He pictured her naked in his bed, her eyes languorous, dark with desire, that long hair spread over the pillow, curling over her shoulder, covering one breast. He saw himself leaning over her, lifting the silken lock, baring a rosy nipple to his gaze, to his eager mouth—

"Know anything, Kirk?" Ramon's voice intruded on his fantasy.

"What?" They were all staring at him. Disgusted with himself, Kirk realized he'd missed the conversation. *Way to go, Butler.* Why did he waste his time dreaming about Tonya Brewster? She was wrong for him. They were from different worlds, realms so far apart they could never meet. He ordered himself to erase those erotic images from his mind, to kill the desire that curled in his gut. He glared at Tonya, redirecting his anger at himself to her.

"Would that cousin of Rick's, the kid you've been working with, know anything about where Rick might be?" Ramon repeated.

"Toby Carson? I doubt it," Kirk answered, getting back to business. "He's still on the fringes of the gang. Damn, I wish I had more time to spend with him, or that the cops around here would find the time to participate in the volunteer program."

"I guess your meeting last week with Captain Morales wasn't a rousing success," Ramon said.

"Total bust," Kirk said, scowling. "He agreed with the concept, nodded his head in all the right places and said he'd mention it to his officers. But the cops in this neighborhood are already involved in so many programs, they can't promise anything. No commitments on a regular basis, anyway.

Ramon nodded glumly. "Bottom line—we can expect zero response."

"Right."

"Damn!" Ladonna's voice shook with anger. "If they'd give us a couple of hours a week, we could work miracles in this neighborhood. It'd pay off in the long run. Less juvenile crime and—"

"Would seven be enough?" Tonya asked suddenly.

Kirk blinked at the interruption. What was she talking about?

Ramon looked confused, too. "Seven...what?" he asked.

"Police officers," Tonya said. "I've rounded up seven guys who are interested in volunteering, and—"

"Girl, are you sayin' you've got seven real live cops— those guys in the uniforms with the badges—who are actually willing to donate some free time here?" Ladonna said.

Tonya nodded. "Is that okay? Is seven too many?"

"Too many?" Ramon laughed. "You just increased our volunteer program three-and-a-half times." He shook his head, obviously disbelieving. "When did this come about?"

"I've heard you mention the program and, well, I talked to some people yesterday."

Yesterday! Kirk stared at her dumbfounded. He'd been trying for six months to get this program off the ground, and she'd done it yesterday? How? *Dumb question.* A woman like Tonya Brewster probably picked up the phone and dialed the chief of police direct. "You must have connections," he told her, a cynical smile curling his lips.

She grinned at him and nodded. "I do. I'll talk to Rusty tomorrow."

Jealousy, as sharp as a knife, stabbed Kirk. "Who's Rusty?" he growled.

Ramon's head jerked around at the tone of Kirk's voice.

Tonya chuckled. "Rusty's the cop in my neighborhood."

The knife blade turned. "You're on a first-name basis with him?" He ignored Ladonna's startled frown, the flash of warning in Ramon's eyes, and stared at Tonya. "How so?" he asked.

"Tickets," Tonya said, her eyes sparkling with humor. "Speeding gets you acquainted with a lot of police. I'm on a first-name basis with most of them."

Tickets. Kirk couldn't help grinning back at her. Tonya Brewster was one surprise after another.

ENCOURAGED BY KIRK'S SMILE, Tonya decided she'd talk to him when the staff meeting ended, but when she jumped up, he was already striding out of the room. She hurried after him, but his long legs had already carried him a good distance down the hall and she would have had to sprint to catch up.

With a shrug, she turned around and headed for her office. She had to conclude that Kirk was deliberately avoiding her. Ever since the afternoon when he'd pulled her into his arms for that searing kiss, he'd gone out of his way to keep from crossing her path. Why? she wondered as she sat behind her desk. Had her kiss disappointed him? No, he'd been as aroused as she. His heart had thudded as wildly as hers; she'd felt it. But maybe he'd had second thoughts.

Tonya propped her chin in her hands. She hated being in the dark, and Kirk Butler seemed a master at leaving her with unanswered questions. In the space of a week, the infernal man had managed to stir up every possible feeling from enmity to desire. Mostly desire. A heaping dose of desire.

And what was she going to do about that?

Sounds from outside distracted her, and she looked out the window. A group of youngsters, Toby Carson among them, trooped past, heading for the basketball court. Was there a game this afternoon? The morning had been rainy, but the sky had cleared, so if a game was scheduled, it could go on as planned.

Tonya opened her drawer and checked the weekly printout she'd picked up in Ramon's office yesterday. Basketball game, four-thirty. She'd promised Germain, the youngster she'd met last week, that she'd watch him play sometime. Why not now?

Besides, Kirk coached the basketball team. Maybe if she went to the game, she'd have a chance to talk to him afterward, find out where they stood. She got up and reached for the jacket—the dull gray jacket—she'd worn this morning. If nothing else, while she watched the game, she'd watch Kirk, too...and enjoy the view.

The view was fabulous, she decided a few minutes later as she perched on the bench and trained her eyes on the man in front of her. He stood talking with a broad-shouldered African American man. Tonya guessed that must be James Watson, the middle school coach who helped out here. He, too, was a well-built man, but Kirk had him beat, hands down.

"Hey, you're back."

Tonya tore her gaze from Kirk's well-crafted buns and smiled up at Germain Parker. The teenager, wearing a basketball uniform—a neutral brown-and-white one, she noticed—radiated energy like a live wire. He gave her a broad grin and a high five. "Get ready," he boasted, dancing on his toes. "We gonna beat those suckers like you never seen, and I'm gonna be the star."

If his enthusiasm was any indication, Tonya believed him. "I'll cheer for you," she told him.

A shrill whistle got Tonya's attention. She turned toward the court and her gaze met Kirk's. His eyes flashed with surprise, dismay. Pleased, Tonya wiggled her fingers in a half wave.

He nodded briefly and turned away, but not before she read the flash of emotion in his eyes. As he strode onto the court, Tonya couldn't suppress a smug smile. He hadn't expected her to be here. And her presence made him uncomfortable. Good.

The whistle sounded again, and Tonya watched Germain swagger onto the court. He glanced over at her and grinned, then focused on the tip-off. His team got possession, and Germain took over, dribbling down the court, dodging one opponent, swerving around another. He passed the ball to Toby and eluded a guard as he raced toward the basket. The ball came back to Germain, he aimed and sent it through the hoop with a satisfying swoosh. Two-zero. Tonya jumped up and cheered.

Despite her enjoyment of Germain's performance, Tonya was distracted by Kirk. His voice as he shouted encouragement to his team, his movements, his very presence commanded her attention. He was like a powerful magnet, drawing her eyes, her thoughts. At times the game vanished from her awareness and she was conscious only of him.

Then a shout would bring her back, and she'd focus on Germain again. He put on a stunning display of athleticism—dribbling, passing, rebounding and outscoring both opponents and teammates. A sheen of sweat dampened his face, his chest heaved with harsh breaths, but his smile never faded. The kid was in heaven. Today he was a star, and he played to the crowd.

Behind Tonya, three girls kept up a running commentary on his performance, punctuated by giggles and exaggerated sighs. "Oh, that Germain. He so-o fast."

"Ooh, girl, he ba-ad." Tonya interpreted the remark to mean the opposite.

Germain must have heard because he wiggled his bottom, then turned and winked at his fans. The girls practically swooned.

When the game ended with a lopsided score of sixty-four to thirty-eight, they scurried over to congratulate Germain and his teammates. Tonya stood and watched them, enjoying the display of hero worship and flirting. Typical teenagers, Tonya thought. How blessedly normal their behavior seemed after the other day's ugly scene with Janene and Rick.

After a few minutes the youngsters drifted away. The girls, chattering excitedly, left the center, and the boys went back inside to change.

As they crossed the yard toward the door, Germain suddenly broke from the group and raced back, coming to a halt in front of Tonya. "What'd you think?" he asked. He knew he'd been good, she was sure, but he wanted to hear her say it.

"You were great. Super."

His grin broadened. "Yeah." Then he dashed over to the azalea bushes, which were just beginning to bloom, broke off a stem and returned to Tonya. With a bow, he presented the flowers. "Thanks for comin'," he told her.

Touched by the gesture, Tonya responded in kind, with a curtsy. "Thank *you* for the flowers," she said.

Germain raised a hand in salute and loped off to join the others.

Tonya smiled after him. Nice kid, she thought. As she

strolled toward the door, she lifted the azalea blossoms to her nose and inhaled the fragrance of approaching spring.

"Wait up." Kirk's gruff voice came from behind her.

Tonya halted. As she waited for him to catch up, her heart began to thud. This was the first time since last week that he'd sought her out. What did he want?

He reached her side, and their eyes met. His were dark and intense. Tonya's throat constricted. "Wh-what?" she croaked.

Kirk glanced behind him, toward the street. "Let's go in."

Tonya nodded. For a moment, she'd forgotten they were in a potentially dangerous area, and it was getting dark. She'd only focused on the fact that they'd played this scene before and had ended up in each other's arms. She wondered if Kirk was remembering the same thing. Her pulse beat in her ears as she breathed in the heady scent of sweat and man.

He opened the door for her, they went inside, passed the spot where they'd stopped last week and continued down the hall. No second act, she thought, then blinked when she realized that Kirk had spoken. "What?"

"I said I saw you out there with Parker."

She frowned. "And?"

"I didn't like what went on."

His voice was edgy, too edgy to suit her. Deliberately, Tonya raised the azaleas and took a long sniff. "What didn't you like?" she asked.

"You encouraged him."

She went dead still. Anger surged where anticipation had bubbled only minutes ago. "*Encouraged* him?" she drawled. "You think I was flirting with the kid?" When Kirk remained silent, she snapped, "Spit it out, Butler. That's what you think, isn't it?"

Kirk took her by the elbow and propelled her along the hall toward her office. In the doorway he stopped. "No, I said 'encouraged' and that's what I meant. Parker is unpredictable. One day he's rookie of the year, the next day he's a demon. The more attention he gets, the more likely he is to act out. I've seen him at his worst, believe me."

She *didn't* believe him. Germain was a kid who needed attention, who craved it. She recognized the signals. Why shouldn't she? She'd transmitted the same ones at his age. "I think you're overreacting," she said, raising her chin. "What I did was good for him. Besides, it was no big deal. Just a harmless gesture."

Kirk's laugh had no mirth. "Harmless? Lady," he growled, "nothing about you is harmless." As Tonya stared, openmouthed, he swung around and stalked away.

She sank down on her chair. "What was that all about?"

Kirk Butler had to be the most infuriating man in the entire universe. One day he kissed her until her toes curled, the next he threatened to bite her head off. And in between, he acted as if she didn't exist.

"What's left?" she muttered. "Where do we go from here?"

7

NOWHERE. APPARENTLY, she and Kirk were going nowhere.

The next day he made himself scarce again. Her only glimpse of him came when she passed the classroom where Ladonna taught childbirth preparation and saw him standing outside, talking to one of the teenage girls. His voice was low, gentle, a marked contrast to the tone he'd used with Tonya. She sighed. Whatever game they were playing, she hadn't figured out the rules.

But she wouldn't let him stop her from doing her job. She had never let a man dictate her life, and she didn't intend to start now.

The next afternoon found her back on the bench by the basketball court. She had a perfect right to be here; she was supposed to evaluate the center's programs and report back to the foundation. And if her presence annoyed Kirk, tough. In fact, she hoped she disturbed him just as much as he did her. She ignored his glowering countenance and settled down to watch practice.

Half a dozen youngsters crowded around Kirk. Toby was there, but Germain was not among them.

A few minutes later, she caught sight of the boy shuffling across the yard, his gaze on the ground. This was a very different Germain from the enthusiastic teenager she'd seen yesterday. Uh-oh, she thought as Kirk's face darkened. "Parker," he shouted. "You're close to being late again."

"Yeah, so what?" Germain's expression was defiant.

"Get over here. Now."

Germain maintained his plodding gait. If anything, he moved slower.

Kirk ignored the boy's obvious challenge. "Shoot around," he barked, and the others took their places.

Germain elbowed his way into the line, shoving one boy out of his way. "Hey, watch it," the kid said.

Germain paid no attention. When his turn came, he grabbed the ball and tossed it against the backboard.

"No rebounds, Parker," Kirk ordered. "We're shooting baskets."

"Oh, yeah, I forgot." He tossed the ball, watched it catch the rim and sail through, then ran back to grab it and shoot again.

Kirk jumped and batted the ball away before it reached the hoop. "One shot apiece."

"Yeah, yeah," Germain muttered.

"Kirk!" Ramon came outside. "Can I see you a minute?"

"Sure. Keep it up, fellas." He strode across the yard and looked at a stack of papers Ramon held out.

The kids continued their practice. Germain paid little attention to his teammates. He picked up two small rocks and began juggling them, punctuating his tosses with exaggerated movements and loud guffaws.

His antics didn't go unnoticed. "What you doin'?" one of the other kids asked. "Practicing to be a clown 'stead of a basketball player?"

"Yeah, why not?" Germain dropped the rocks and broke into a dance step.

"Man, you crazy."

"You got that right," Germain agreed.

Tonya glanced nervously at Kirk. Should she go back and get him? Germain seemed out of control today. Eyeing the court, she slid over toward the other end of the bench.

Germain's turn came and he swaggered up to the basket, tossed the ball from hand to hand, threw it in and caught it after one bounce. Then, with a glance toward Kirk and Ramon, he spun around, executing a perfect shot over his shoulder. "Four points," he chortled.

Some of his teammates glared; others snickered.

Germain didn't seem to care either way. He strolled to the end of the line, stood a moment toying with a button on his sweater, then suddenly pushed forward and cut in line ahead of Toby. Clearly offended, the other boy shoved him.

"You keep your hands offa me," Germain snarled, adding an obscenity that had Toby clenching his fists and taking a threatening step forward.

"Get him, Toby," someone shouted.

Germain darted away. He was fast, but Toby's pace was fueled by anger. He easily overtook Germain and landed the first punch. Tonya winced at the sound of fist connecting with jaw.

The other boys yelled encouragement. "Come on, Toby. Get that little—"

Terrified, Tonya jumped up. "Kirk," she shouted, and ran for him.

But the noise had already alerted him. He charged past Tonya with Ramon close behind him. Before Kirk reached them, Germain had Toby on the ground and was straddling his chest and pummeling him unmercifully.

Kirk grabbed Germain from behind and jerked him to his feet while Ramon pulled Toby up and walked him to the other side of the court. Shouting curses, Germain reared back and kicked. But Kirk was too strong; he easily held Germain away from him and soon had him subdued. "Inside, Parker," he ordered. "I'll see you in my office."

Germain clenched his fists. "What about him?" he snarled, scowling at Toby.

"He's not your concern. Get inside."

Germain swore violently. "No way. I'm gettin' off the team. You ain't my coach no more so you can't tell me what to do. I'm goin' home." He stomped away.

Maybe she could get through to him, Tonya thought. She'd talk him into listening to Kirk, staying on the team. As he stalked by her, she put out a hand. "Germain."

"Leave me be." With another curse, he pushed past her. She watched in silence as he marched across the yard, bent to pick something up, then disappeared around the side of the building.

She took a step after him, then another, but Ramon's voice stopped her. "Let him go. Give him time to calm down."

Tonya swung around. She'd been so focused on Germain, she hadn't heard Ramon come up behind her. Now she glanced back at the basketball court and saw Kirk talking to Toby. "Sit out for three minutes," Kirk told him, and gestured to the bench. Toby plodded over and sat down. Kirk blew his whistle and the rest of the boys gathered around him to continue their practice.

Tonya didn't like the way Kirk had handled the fight. She turned and looked toward the front of the building. Maybe Germain had had second thoughts. No, he was gone. And Ramon was right. She could do nothing for the boy now. But as she thought of the angry, defiant youngster marching off, she felt a lump in her throat.

"Come on." Ramon's voice was sympathetic. "You look like you could use some coffee."

Tonya nodded and fell into step beside him. In a way, this was worse than the scene between Rick and Janene for Tonya because she *knew* Germain. She'd developed a relationship with the boy, at least she'd thought so. Now she didn't know what to think. She was upset and disgusted with Kirk. If anything, he'd made Germain angrier.

When they arrived at the kitchen, Ramon filled a mug with coffee and held it out. Tonya took it, but her hand shook so badly that liquid sloshed onto the counter. Embarrassed, she set the cup down.

"Why don't you sit down?" Ramon asked gently.

"No, I'm okay," she said, though tears stung her eyes and her hand wouldn't stop shaking. She leaned against the counter and looked at Ramon. How could he be so calm? "Is it...is it always like this here?"

"Violent? Yeah, a lot of the time it is."

"It's a violent neighborhood."

Tonya looked up to see Kirk in the doorway. Without a thought, she lit into him. "You played favorites out there."

"You know I didn't," he said quietly, firmly. "You saw Germain start it."

"Yeah," she conceded, "but Toby's your boy. You gave him three minutes on the bench, but you sent Germain inside."

With a sigh, Kirk went to the coffeepot, filled a cup and took a sip. "I call 'em like I see 'em. That's the best I can do." He ran his fingers through his already tousled hair. "Maybe you're right. Maybe I do give preference to Toby, but damn it, the kid has so much going for him. His grades are good. He could get into college *if* he keeps them up, *if* he stays out of the gang..." He sighed again. "So many ifs."

Now Tonya saw the frustration on his face, the lines of fatigue and discouragement, and forgot her own anger and shock. Suddenly, she wanted to put her arms around him, draw his head down to her breast and tell him everything would be all right.

But it wouldn't.

How did he and Ramon and the others bear it? How did

they deal with these kids day after day? She raised her eyes to Kirk's and found him looking at her. "How do you get used to it?" she asked softly.

"You don't, but you harden yourself. You build a wall, like a doctor does to handle the death of patients."

"But—"

"Go home, Tonya. It's getting late." She heard none of the anger he'd expressed before when he'd told her to leave, only a resigned sympathy.

Tonya nodded. For once, she was willing to take his advice.

She left the kitchen and stopped by her office to retrieve her purse. She opened it and felt for her keys. Damn things were hiding somewhere. She shook the bag. Yes, she could hear them rattling around on the bottom, but when she stuck her hand in, they were nowhere to be found.

With a resigned sigh, she sat down and dumped the bag out on her desk. A tube of lipstick rolled onto the floor, a telephone message she'd carelessly stuffed inside and hadn't been able to find appeared. She fished through the rest of the clutter until she located the keys. She tossed everything else back in the bag, got up and remembered the lipstick.

Finding it took several minutes of crawling around on the floor. After peering at the label on the bottom of the tube, she dropped the lipstick in the trash can. That tube was empty, and she'd forgotten to replace it. Annoyed, she groped in her purse until she found the notebook with her daily schedule. Under Things To Do, she scribbled, "Buy lipstick," then on the next line added, "Get organized." Nice trick if she could do it. So far in all her twenty-seven years, she hadn't come close.

She flipped off the light in her office and locked the door. At least the hunt for her keys had gotten her mind off Germain. Maybe she'd stop by Sam and Wade's tonight. Her cousins, especially Wade, were always good for a laugh. Or maybe, since they too dealt with the seamy side of life in their detective agency, they could give her some pointers on how to build that tough shell Kirk mentioned.

She left by the back door and walked rapidly to the parking lot, humming to herself. She'd call Sam on the cellular phone she kept hidden under the front seat of the truck, offer to stop and pick up dinner—

"Oh, my God!"

She stood and stared for a moment, hoping she was imagining what she thought she saw, praying that the stress of the afternoon had brought on a hallucination. Then she raced to the truck. No, this was no illusion. What she saw was real.

Someone had smashed the passenger-side window of the pickup to smithereens.

She stared down at the ground. Shards of glass glittered in the waning sunlight. The entire window was gone. Inside she saw more bits of shattered glass on the seat and floorboard.

Carefully, she opened the door and peered in. Had anything been taken? Nothing. They hadn't even tried to force open the glove compartment. That was some consolation, but what an end to the day!

Should she call the cops? No, she doubted it would do much good. What she needed to do was get something with which to sweep up the glass. There went her plans for the evening.

She dashed inside, got a whisk broom, dustpan and garbage bag from the kitchen closet and headed back down the hall, her mind focused on the broken window.

With a thunk, she collided against a warm, very hard

body. She heard a sharp breath and inhaled a familiar scent. Kirk.

Tonya gasped and dropped the broom as he reached out to steady her. Darn, she didn't want to see him now. He'd probably deliver a lecture about the window and manage to make her feel like the culprit herself.

"Where are you going in such a hurry?" he asked.

She wouldn't lie, she decided; she'd just evade the truth. "Home."

He raised a brow. "With a broom?"

"I guess you wouldn't believe me if I said it was my transportation."

He shook his head slowly, then gave her that sexy smile. "Oh, I believe you're a witch, but not the kind who rides on broomsticks."

Intrigued, Tonya asked, "What kind?"

"The kind who casts spells on mortal men." His voice was low and deep, like rough velvet. He bent his head. Lifting a hand to her cheek, he urged her closer.

Tonya's eyes drifted shut. Her lips parted—

"Coach! Someone bashed in the window of that black pickup out there!" Like a bucket of ice water tossed in their faces, the excited voice broke the spell.

Kirk straightened. "Black pickup?" His gaze shot to the broom, then to Tonya's face. "Yours, right?"

"Mine," she muttered, and braced for the inevitable lecture.

To her surprise, Kirk merely picked up the broom and said, "Thanks for telling me, Terrell. We'll take care of it."

They went out into the gathering dusk. As she gazed for the second time at the smashed window, Tonya sighed. "Thank heavens my baby's safe at home."

Kirk glanced at her quickly, startled.

Tonya realized how her words would be interpreted and laughed. "I mean my baby in the garage."

"You have a baby in your garage?" he asked, looking totally confused.

"I mean my car—the Jaguar. I'm glad *it* wasn't damaged."

"Ah." He chuckled. "Has anyone ever mentioned that you're hard to follow?"

"Yes, I mean, no. Give me the broom." She pulled it away from him and began to sweep. Kirk leaned against the front fender and watched her. "Would one of the Sabers do this?" she asked him.

He shook his head. "I doubt it. Too tame. More likely, Germain did it."

"Germain!" Tonya stopped sweeping and stared at him, astonished. "He...he wouldn't."

"Wouldn't he? You saw him during basketball practice."

"Yeah, he was on a tear today. But yesterday—"

"Every day's different with Germain," Kirk said. "You never know what to expect from him. He's a kid with an attitude. The only thing you can be sure of is that when he has one of these angry outbursts, he'll do just about anything. That kid's headed for serious trouble."

"You mean crime." Tonya emptied a dustpan of glass into the garbage bag, then straightened and put her hands on her hips. It was a gesture anyone in her family would recognize—Tonya at her most determined. "We can't stand around and let that happen. We have to do something."

"Don't you think we've tried? Nothing works." He sighed as she advanced toward him. "Okay, I'll talk to him again tomorrow."

"What time?"

"In the after—" He frowned. "You don't need to be there."

"Yes, I do."

"Tonya, believe me. Everyone has talked to this boy and no one's gotten anywhere."

"I'd like to try." Seeing a no forming on his lips, she added, "Please. It's important to me."

"Why?"

Because he reminds me of myself at that age, she thought, remembering her early adolescence. One day she'd feel euphoric and the next day even a look would ignite her temper and she'd mouth off at teachers or her parents. Of course, she'd never resorted to vandalism, though maybe if she'd grown up in a different environment, one like Germain's, she'd have become a delinquent. But she had no intention of dredging up her past and presenting it for Kirk's scrutiny, so she said, "I'm interested in Germain. Maybe I can help."

Kirk shrugged. "Suit yourself, but remember, he's unpredictable."

"Okay." Tonya opened the driver's door and, with the whisk, began brushing glass off the seat and into the bag. "How are you going to get Germain over here to talk?" she asked.

"I'm not even going to try. We'll set something up at his school. I know the principal."

"That's handy. Do you think you can get Germain's family to come, too?"

"I doubt it. His dad's been out of the picture for years, and I've met his mother." Tonya heard the disgust in his voice. "She's pretty much washed her hands of him."

"But...but he's just a kid."

"He's big enough to bash in your window."

She couldn't argue with that. She worked silently for a few minutes, then surveyed the seat. "There, I think that's it." She slammed the door. "Ow!"

Kirk was at her side in an instant. "What happened?"

"Nothing serious. I must've had some glass stuck to my hand."

"Let me see." Kirk took her hand and turned it over. They both stared at the crisscross of tiny cuts. "You're bleeding," he said, his voice thick.

Amused, Tonya said, "I don't think it's fatal." Then she glanced up at him and saw his pale face. "Hey, a macho guy like you doesn't faint at the sight of blood, does he?"

He sent a disgusted and very male scowl her way. "No. Go wash your hands. I'll finish up."

Tonya couldn't resist teasing. "Sweeping's women's work."

He grabbed the broom and muttered something unpleasant under his breath. Laughing despite her smarting hand, Tonya went inside. In the bright light of the rest room she could see tiny slivers of glass on her palm. She washed carefully, wincing at the sting. As she rinsed her hands, she thought about Germain.

When she returned to the parking lot, Kirk looked up from tying the garbage bag. "Are you okay?"

"Fine. You know," she added, "I thought about what you said about being careful around Germain. I will, but I'm sure it's unnecessary. He took out his anger on the car. He wouldn't hurt me."

"Wouldn't he?" Kirk's voice was low, angry. He grabbed her hand and turned it palm up. "He already has."

To Tonya's astonishment, he bent his head and very slowly, very gently brushed his lips over her hand. Though his breath warmed her tender skin, she felt a shiver race up her spine.

Then her bones dissolved as his mouth traveled to her wrist and his tongue touched her pulse. She gasped. At the sound, he raised his head.

For a long moment, they stared at each other. He put his hands on her shoulders and urged her closer.

She wasn't sure she was ready for this. She wasn't sure about anything. Legs trembling, Tonya stepped away. She slipped a hand behind her and fumbled with the door handle. "I...I should go." *Ask me to stay.*

But he said nothing, only went to unlock the gate, then returned to the side of the truck. He stood for a moment, still silent, then, in a voice that was not quite steady, said, "Put something on your hand when you get home."

"Okay." She had to try twice before her shaking fingers could fit the key into the ignition.

My God. She'd had her first kiss at age eleven when Tommy Benning had pecked her cheek in the lunch line right under the surprised eyes of Mrs. McLanahan, the fifth-grade teacher. Since then, she'd kissed and been kissed more times than she could count. But never like this. Just the touch of his lips—on her *palm*, for heaven's sake— and she'd melted like butter. The man should come with a sign: Danger. Proceed With Caution."

She watched him in the rearview mirror as she drove away from the parking lot. He stood like a statue, a be-mused expression on his face. She remembered once on a trip to Athens, she'd visited the National Museum and seen a statue of some Greek god. Deep-set eyes, perfect phy-sique, rippling muscles. Standing in the darkness, Kirk re-minded her of the statue, but *it* was lifeless marble and *he* was hot flesh. She still trembled from his touch, his kiss. She was tempted to make a U-turn, go back to the center and...

"Never mind," she said aloud. She shouldn't be thinking like that. A rumble of thunder got her attention. She should be thinking about...the weather.

Glancing one last time at Kirk standing by the gate, she wondered what *he* was thinking.

KIRK CURSED HIMSELF roundly. He'd done it, given in to the craving to taste her again. Seeing the broken window had started it. He'd thought about how much worse the situation could have been. That damn kid could have come at Tonya instead of her truck. When he'd seen the blood on her hand, he'd gone a little crazy. If she hadn't defused the situation by making a joke of it, he might have been fool enough to...he wasn't sure what.

He should have left things as they were, but no, he'd had to kiss her. Her hand, of all things. Why? He wasn't given to courtly gestures. He damn well wasn't a gentleman.

Disgusted with himself, he swiped at a rock with the broom. Did she have any idea how she affected him? If he hadn't used every ounce of control, he'd have gone off like a rocket, taken her right there on the concrete parking lot or dragged her in the building like a caveman.

He snorted. *Caveman.* That's probably what she thought he was. A woman like her was used to finesse, to the kind of men who wore tailored suits to work, who had Ivy League educations and Old Money connections, who knew how to court a woman gently. Guys like that made him want to puke.

And since the debacle with Amelia, he'd learned to steer clear of women like Tonya. Women who belonged to the country club and drove red Jaguars. Unfortunately, that didn't stop him from wanting her. All he had to do was look at her, hear her voice, and his response made his jeans feel as if they'd shrunk two sizes. Damn, he was still aroused. Too bad the basketball court was dark. He needed some exercise.

He went in and retrieved his motorcycle. As he pushed it outside, he glanced at the sky. Lightning sliced through the clouds. Thunder sounded off to the east. If the rain didn't cool him off by the time he got home, he'd go to the gym and do some sit-ups and some push-ups...and some bench presses...and swim a few laps.

By the time Tonya got through with him, he'd look like Mr. Universe.

8

IN DEFERENCE TO the school visit, Tonya wore a suit. She fidgeted with the calf-length skirt as she got ready to leave her office; she'd become accustomed to the comfort of jeans. As she hurried down the hall to meet Kirk, she wondered if he'd wear a suit, too.

He didn't, but he had dressed up for the occasion in a shirt and sport jacket. He wore his usual belt with the big silver buckle, and jeans that molded his muscular thighs like a second skin. Her gaze, which seemed to have a mind of its own, fastened on those thighs. When she realized he'd noticed, she raised her eyes and focused on his belt buckle. Mistake—she'd chosen another dangerous region. She quickly glanced up, then looked away, but not before she caught the knowing look on his face. Her cheeks heated.

Talk about the meeting with Germain, she instructed herself, and cleared her throat. "Shall we walk to the school?"

"I'd rather not, with Rick still on the loose. Besides, it's going to storm. And I won't be able to take us, either," he added, his gaze skimming over her legs. "You're not dressed for a ride on a Harley."

She couldn't argue with that. It had been raining off and on since last night, and puddles filled the streets. She didn't care to get drenched driving through them on a motorcycle, Tonya thought as she tried to discreetly smooth her skirt. With Kirk's eyes following her every move, it was impossible. She gave up and said, "We'll take the pickup."

"You've been driving it without a window?" His voice registered disapproval.

Did he think she was a complete idiot? "Of course not," she huffed. "I had the window replaced. The repair shop delivered the truck at noon."

He tucked a bulky manila folder under his arm. "Let's go, then."

Tonya slipped on a jacket as they went outside. The sky was still overcast, the wind chilly. In spite of the azaleas blooming in the yard, winter had apparently returned. "Did you talk to Germain's mother about coming?" Tonya asked as they headed for the truck.

"Yeah, she declined the invitation. No surprise there."

"With the mother he has, it's no surprise he acts the way he does," Tonya said in disgust.

"Don't lay all the blame on his mother. The kid has a violent streak, and he'd be in hot water no matter what."

Tonya halted and swung around to face him. Hands on her hips, she glared at him. "What do you mean? That he can't change—he's on a path for life?"

"I wouldn't be working with these kids if I thought that. I'm saying once they develop a taste for mischief, it gets harder to change them. Look at Rick."

Tonya shuddered. She didn't want Germain to end up like Rick—violent, mean, no doubt behind bars someday. "Then we have to do something now."

"You look like you're ready to call out the marines," he said, and smiled. The smile that signaled danger. His voice lowered. "Your eyes glitter when you get worked up."

Flustered, she didn't know what to say. She looked around and realized they'd crossed the parking lot. She took a nervous step back and bumped into the truck.

Kirk moved closer, reminding her again of a tiger. And he was on the prowl again. "You're blushing."

She fumbled for her purse. "Watch out. I have my weapon."

Raising both hands above his head, he grinned and stepped back. "I wouldn't want to tangle with that battering ram again. What do you keep in it?"

"Essentials."

"I'll bet," he said, opening the door for her. He walked around to the passenger side and climbed in. "I know you have an alarm in there. My ears are still ringing. What other essentials?"

"You want a list? There's keys, makeup, a billfold, my daily schedule." She continued reciting as she drove. "A pocket dictionary and a poker deck."

He chuckled. "It's a wonder you don't have a hernia."

"It's not so bad."

"So, do you play poker in your spare time?" he asked.

"Sometimes. Or solitaire, or gin rummy."

"We'll have to have a game," he said, giving her a lazy smile laced with challenge. It made her tingle all over.

She pulled into the Franklin D. Roosevelt Middle School parking lot and glanced around. The school looked like her old middle school. Ugly red brick. Front lawn covered with feeble grass and healthy weeds. American and Texas flags flapping noisily in the wind.

A couple of teenage boys hung out a third-floor window. One of them leaned out farther and let out a long wolf whistle. Tonya ignored him.

Kirk chuckled softly. That she didn't ignore. "Wipe the smirk off your face," she muttered, eliciting another chuckle. She'd make a note to wear baggy slacks next time she made a school visit.

The office was near the front door. Barely glancing up when they entered, a tired-looking secretary thrust a signin sheet at them. Dutifully, they wrote their names, then Kirk asked for Karen Monroe, the principal.

When Ms. Monroe walked in, Tonya had to stifle a gasp. Had the breed of principals she'd known died out? She remembered the school administrators from her childhood—gray-haired, middle-aged ladies with bifocals perched on their noses, their bodies concealed in shapeless suits.

This principal had fiery auburn hair, jade green eyes and a body that belonged on "Baywatch." If Tonya merited a wolf whistle, this woman must evoke jungle howls.

Ms. Monroe's eyes lit up when she saw Kirk. How well did they know each other? Tonya wondered.

"Hello, Karen," he said.

"Kirk, nice to see you," she said in a low, silky voice. She put out her hand and, according to Tonya's count, left it in Kirk's two seconds too long.

"Karen, this is Tonya Brewster," he said.

"Hello, Ms. Monroe."

"Dr. Monroe," Kirk corrected.

Oh, nice. A sex goddess with a doctorate. Tonya glared at Dr. Monroe's back as they followed her into her office. As she sat down, Tonya noticed a certificate on the wall indicating that the principal had placed in the top five for her age group in this year's Tenneco Marathon. Was there no end to her talents?

And what was her relationship with Kirk? Personal or professional? Eyeing the file cabinet across from the desk, Tonya wondered if he'd ever backed Karen up against it and kissed her senseless, then strolled off without a second glance.

"So you're here to see Germain Parker," Dr. Monroe said. "What's going on?"

Briefly, Kirk described the previous afternoon.

Karen Monroe sighed and made a note in a folder that

lay open on her desk. "This is typical conduct for Germain. I'll put him on the list to see the counselor."

Why hadn't she done that already if she knew about his behavior? Tonya wondered, but she held her tongue.

"He's quite capable," Karen continued as she rummaged through the folder. "His achievement scores last year were above average. Despite what the scores indicate," Karen went on, "Germain's grades are poor. He's failing three subjects. I worry that he's in danger of dropping out of school."

"Are the gangs recruiting him?" Kirk asked.

"No, even for them his behavior's too erratic."

"He's an excellent athlete," Kirk said thoughtfully.

"I wasn't aware of that," Karen said, looking interested.

"Sports might keep him in school."

"Now there's an idea!" Karen looked at Kirk as if he'd come up with a solution to end the federal deficit. Tonya wanted to gag. "Track season's beginning. I'll speak to the coach." She jotted down another note. "Now, you two need a place to meet with the boy. Come along." She led them to a small room down the hall. "This is used for testing, but our diagnostician's out today. I'll send someone for Germain. When you finish, I'd like to know what happened."

They waited in silence until Germain appeared at the door. When he saw them, his eyes widened. A mixture of embarrassment and apprehension passed over his face.

"Sit down, Germain," Kirk said.

"Whatcha want with me?" he asked, nervousness replaced with his usual defiance.

"To talk about two problems. The fight on the court and the broken window."

"Yeah, I was fighting. So what?" He directed his gaze at the wall. "But I don't know nothin' about no window."

Kirk shook his head. "When Ms. Brewster went back to her truck—"

Germain's head shot around. "It was your truck?"

"No, I borrowed it from my cousin. I had to have his window replaced." When Germain's gaze dropped to his shoes, she added softly, "Why'd you do it?"

He shuffled his feet. "I dunno. I had a bad day at school and I jus' got mad. If I'da known it was yours..."

"Windows cost money," Kirk said.

"I don't have no money."

"Maybe you could earn it," Tonya suggested. In spite of his actions, her heart went out to the boy. He looked so miserable.

"Ain't nobody gonna give me a job."

"I will," Tonya said. "You can work at the OK Center in the afternoons until you pay off the window. But I don't want any fights. Or any other mischief."

Beside her, she heard a movement. She turned and glanced at Kirk. His fists were clenched. His eyes were as stormy as the skies outside, and the storm seemed to be directed at her. Why? She didn't have a clue, but she'd worry about it later. Ignoring Kirk, she met Germain's eyes.

He looked away, shuffled his feet. Tonya watched him weigh his options, then decide he had none. "Okay," he mumbled.

"Good," she said. "You can start tomorrow."

Eyes wary, Germain turned to Kirk.

"You'll be off the team for a week," Kirk told him. "After that, you're on trial. If you get to practice on time and keep yourself under control, we'll talk."

"Yes, sir."

Kirk dismissed him and waited for him to shut the door before he turned to Tonya. "Who the hell gave you the right to hire him to work at the center?" he said, his voice low and fierce.

"I... No one."

"Didn't you think of discussing your idea with me?" he asked.

"N-no, it just came to me."

"Like a bolt from the blue."

She lifted her chin. "Exactly."

"Well, next time you get one of those inspirations, you talk it over with me first." He rose, his hands still tightly fisted. He looked even bigger this afternoon, as if his anger had added to his stature. "You're overseeing a grant, not running the show."

So that was it. Suddenly she understood him. His behavior, so confusing up till now, made sense. They were engaged in a power struggle, he and she. A power struggle she hadn't even been aware existed until now. But it was real to Kirk. In his mind she had the upper hand because she had control of the grant, and he resented it. And her. He didn't want to give up an ounce of his authority, and she'd just encroached on his territory.

Arguing would only make things worse. The only way to handle this was to surrender some of her power. Which was easy because it wasn't particularly important to her. She cared more about other things—making a contribution to the center, doing something she could finally be proud of.

"I should have asked," she said. "Sometimes I act without thinking." She saw the surprise on his face and knew she'd said the right thing. "Should we call Germain back in here and work out a different way for him to pay for the window?"

"Leave it," he muttered. "But next time—"

"Next time we'll talk things over."

He nodded. "Let's go back to the office. While you sign us out, I'll run in and tell Karen what happened."

Tonya drew a breath as she followed Kirk into the office. She'd averted a disaster. And now that she had a clearer picture of Kirk, maybe they could...

Establish a better working relationship?

Well, that, too. But at the moment, Tonya's goals were much more personal. She watched as Kirk and Karen Monroe stood talking in the open doorway of the principal's office. She hoped Karen didn't have any designs on Kirk. If she did, Tonya would make sure she would be disappointed.

KIRK STARED AT TONYA as they walked down the hall to the front door of the school. Her face wore a secretive half smile. Whatever she was thinking about, she was enjoying it.

She was something! She'd surprised him again, admitting that her job offer to Germain had been too hasty, that she should have talked it over with Kirk first. He had to respect her for admitting her mistake. Add that to the things he'd grown to like about her and the list was getting damn long. He thought of her liveliness, her grit, her determination. And the fact that she drove him crazy with desire. Man, some list.

Smiling to himself, he opened the door and followed Tonya out. A light rain was falling. Kirk glanced up as they hurried to the truck. "We're going to have a storm," he remarked, gesturing toward the pewter gray clouds to the east, "and it's moving in fast."

His prediction was right. Before they were halfway back to the center, the heavens burst open. Violently. While thunder rumbled, a deluge poured down on them. Rain drummed on the roof, and he had to shout to make himself heard. "Slow down."

Tonya didn't answer. Instead, she maneuvered the truck like a speedboat. Water spewed up, almost to the windows. "Hey—" Kirk leaned over to shout in her ear "—slow this baby down or I'll do it."

He edged his booted foot toward the pedals. Tonya glanced at it and pumped the brake herself. After a minute, she asked, "How are you getting home?"

"My bike."

"In this rain? You won't make it around the corner. Besides, you'll get pneumonia."

"Then I'll hang around the center until the storm's over."

"By the looks of the sky, the rain's going to last all night. I'll take you home."

He wouldn't turn down the chance to spend an extra hour with her. He shrugged. "All right. Want me to drive?" Tonya aimed a disgusted look at him and he grinned. "Okay, let's see how you manage."

"I manage just fine," she muttered. "Why, once when I sat out a hurricane in Puerto Rico, I drove a jeep through San Juan in floodwaters up to your a—abdomen," she corrected.

"I bet."

She lifted her chin. "It's true. Don't you believe—"

"Holy Moses!" Kirk grabbed for the steering wheel as they narrowly missed slamming into a van. "Watch where you're going!"

Her chin rose another notch. "I was."

Kirk shook his head. He'd known driving home with her would be exciting. He hadn't guessed it would be terrifying. "One thing I believe is your collection of traffic tickets. Lady, you are a road hazard."

"It's all relative," Tonya said. "My cousin Stuart once

thought of becoming a race car driver. Now *he* is a danger behind the wheel. I could tell you stories..."

"No, thanks. Is that the cousin who owns the truck?"

"No, *he's* into another kind of adventure." She didn't elaborate but smiled to herself as if she knew a secret.

Kirk wondered what her secret was and what it would be like to unravel all her mysteries. He'd start with her skin. Was it as petal soft all over as on her cheeks? Would it heat from his kisses? Damn, his jeans were getting tight again. He shifted uncomfortably. To distract himself, he returned to the topic of her cousin. "What kind of adventure?"

"Literary."

Literary adventure sounded like an oxymoron to Kirk. And why would a literary type drive a pickup truck? "And did your other cousin become a race car driver?"

"Nope, a banker."

"I have trouble picturing any cousin of yours as a conservative banker."

"Oh, his interest in race car driving was a form of temporary insanity. He gave up the idea by the time he was in college, although he still drives like a maniac. Sad," she said with a mischievous smile, "that's the only thing left of his youthful dreams." Kirk chuckled. "In fact," she continued, "most of my family is very traditional, except Sam, of course. And me. I'm the black sheep."

"Why is that?"

"Too many job changes. No goals." Although she smiled as she spoke, he heard something in her voice that told him her black-sheep status wasn't as funny to her as she pretended. It also explained a lot of things, such as why she stubbornly refused to leave the OK Center, even in the face of teenage violence. She was trying to change her image.

He wondered why her grandfather had sent her to the

center in the first place. As a punishment? As a learning experience? "Why no goals?" he asked.

She shrugged as she plowed past a sedately moving car. "I'm easily bored, I guess. Short attention span."

He'd keep that in mind, he decided. Then a roar of thunder claimed his attention, and he flipped on the radio, pushing buttons until he found a weather report.

It didn't sound good. But he didn't need the radio to tell him that. He'd lived nearly all his life in Houston and knew how flood-prone the city was. With the rain they'd had in the last few days soaking the ground and overflowing the bayous, plus the amount they were getting this afternoon, the city would be waist-deep in water within the hour.

In fact, the water was high enough already that the truck was barely making progress. "Pull over," he directed as they approached a corner.

But he was too late. She was already into the intersection. Water rose along the side of the small truck as the street dipped lower. Then a bus lumbered up beside them. Waves sloshed against the door, drenched the windows. The truck rocked back and forth. "God," Tonya muttered. "I'm getting seasick. I feel like we're on an ocean liner."

"Let's hope it's not the *Titanic*."

They inched across the intersection. The bus pulled ahead. In its wake, a tidal wave washed over the windshield. From the street to their right, a delivery truck plowed into the intersection.

Kirk reached over and pounded on the horn. The truck kept coming. "He's lost his brakes," he shouted to Tonya. "Move it!"

That was one thing she did well. Heedless of the flood, she sped the rest of the way across the intersection. The truck missed them by inches.

She swung into the parking lot on the corner. "No

brakes," she muttered, dodging a car, then another, finally sliding to a stop. When she turned to Kirk, her eyes were filled with devilry. "That was exciting."

"Exciting? A bus nearly sinks us. A truck almost rams us. Your transmission is probably on its last gasp. Lady, if you thought that was fun, you are certifiable."

Tonya leaned back and grinned. "Probably."

He couldn't help smiling back.

"Looks like we're stuck for a while," Tonya said, glancing out of the window.

Kirk nodded. If she wanted her cousin's transmission to survive, they'd have to sit out the storm. He'd experienced enough of Houston's frequent floods to know how many foolhardy drivers had to abandon their cars because they'd tried to drive through water. Once the rain stopped and the overloaded sewer system began to function again, the streets would drain and they could make it home. In the meantime...

"What shall we do to pass the time?" Tonya asked. Her tongue peeped out to moisten her lips, and several ideas crossed his mind. Before he could mention them, she said, "I know. Let's have a picnic."

Would she never stop surprising him? "A *what?*"

"In case you hadn't noticed, we're in a supermarket parking lot. And I'm starving."

"In case *you* hadn't noticed, it's raining."

"No problem," she said airily. "I have an umbrella." She reached under the seat and pulled out a large umbrella. Kirk took it from her and opened the door.

He stepped into water almost as high as the tops of his boots. When he looked back, he saw that Tonya had scrambled across along the bench seat and was on the passenger side, ready to climb out. "You can't walk through this," he said. "Your shoes have holes."

"Yes, they're sandals." She scooted closer to the door. "I can get there if you can."

Damn, she really meant to get out. "If you insist on coming along..." He thrust the umbrella at her and scooped her up in his arms. She squealed and the lady in a nearby car rolled down the window and peered out.

Tonya smiled and waved at her. "It's okay."

She held the umbrella over them, cuddling against his chest, laughing, as he carried her through the storm. Despite the rain, the thunder, the water sloshing into his boots, he enjoyed every soggy step. Her warm breath tickled his cheek, her soft breasts pressed against him. He could have walked like this for miles.

When he set her down inside the store, she tossed her hair back and grinned at him. "You're a knight in shining armor, Butler. Sir Walter Raleigh in modern dress."

He put an arm around her shoulder and pulled her close. "The water was too deep for a cloak."

"This was much better. Now, onward to the salad bar."

They selected salads, pasta, a loaf of crusty sourdough bread and canned drinks. He carried her back to the truck and they spread their picnic on the seat between them. Tonya clinked her soda can against his. "To rainy-day picnics."

"Have you had many?" he asked, envy of other men she might have picnicked with churning through him.

"Oh, yes. On rainy days when my brother and I were kids and we'd whine about not being able to go out to play, Mom would spread an old blanket on the floor and we'd have indoor picnics." She smiled as if she could see that childhood scene. "We'd make peanut butter and jelly sandwiches and play Battle or Go Fish, and sometimes we'd tell ghost stories. Ryan, my brother, could tell stories that would scare you silly."

He envied that even more—the warm, loving family she described. A mother around to make sandwiches, a brother to play games with. His own family hadn't been like Germain's, but it was a far cry from Tonya's. They'd grown up in different worlds. They still lived in different worlds.

He reached for the radio dial. "Let's hear the weather report," he said gruffly.

"Flooding is causing massive traffic tie-ups throughout the Greater Houston area. Rain is expected to continue for the next several hours…"

"Guess we'll be here awhile." When they finished their meal, Tonya gathered up the plastic containers and stuffed them in the grocery sack, then reached for her purse. She fished inside for her deck of cards and a jingling coin purse, then looked up at him. Her lips curved in a slow, beguiling smile; her eyes gleamed wickedly. "Poker or gin?" The way she said them, even the names of the card games sounded sexy.

Kirk's stomach lurched. "Poker," he said hoarsely.

Her smile widened. "My choice, too."

"Think you're good, huh?"

Her lashes fluttered. "An ace. What about you?" Her eyes raked over him. "Are you good?"

Somehow he didn't think they were talking about poker anymore. He took the cards from her hand and shuffled them expertly. "You can let me know…afterward. Cut."

He dealt the cards and watched Tonya scrutinize her hand and discard three. She pursed her lips and considered, counted out ten pennies and tossed them on the seat. "Each one's worth a dollar. Ten."

He found his wallet, raised her ten, and the battle was on.

He liked listening to her mutter to herself under her breath. Liked the way she narrowed her eyes as if she could see right through his cards. Liked hearing her chatter. "I learned to play poker at my grandfather's knee," she remarked. "Why, once when we were in Las Vegas and I was only seven, I sat in his lap at the poker table and helped him win fifty grand."

"Have you ever entered a liar's contest?" Kirk asked, realizing that he simply liked being with her. She made him laugh.

And, God, she made him want.

As they played, the space inside the truck seemed to shrink, the air seemed to heat. Unspoken sexual messages flew back and forth. The windows of the truck fogged, and he could swear it was as much from what was going on between them as from the weather. Their fingers brushed, their gazes met, slid away and met again; their voices lowered, softened. He wanted, waited. And wondered how much longer he could do without her.

Outside, the sky darkened; Tonya flipped on the light as rain slowed to a patter. "That's eight hundred dollars for you, seven-sixty for me."

"We'll call it a draw."

"Okay. Do you know any other games?" He shook his head. "Card tricks?"

He picked up the deck. "Yeah, I can make them disappear." He'd waited as long as he could. No more. He tossed the cards over his shoulder, turned off the light and reached for her. "Come here, Tonya."

Without hesitation, she moved into his arms. For a moment, he only held her, savoring. "You feel so good," he whispered.

"So do you."

He ran teasing kisses along her jaw. "You smell good, too...but different."

"I changed perfume."

With his tongue, he explored her ear and was delighted when she shivered. "Why?"

She drew back and looked at him, her eyes full of mischief. "Wearing the same one every day would be boring. Don't you like surprises?"

"Mmm, *yes*." He groaned and pulled her back to him.

Then he forgot about talking, forgot everything but the need that consumed him. His hands dived into the silk of her hair, his tongue plundered the honey of her mouth. She sighed; he moaned. When she twined her arms around his neck, he lifted her into his lap. His teeth scraped along her neck, his hand slipped beneath her jacket and covered her breast.

"You're so soft," he muttered, fumbling with buttons.

"Kirk." She pushed against his chest.

He opened his eyes. Half-drunk from her taste, he stared at her, uncomprehending.

"Not here," she whispered urgently. "Not now." She scrambled back into the driver's seat.

Of course, not here. Of course, not now.

Around them, headlights were coming on. Horns were honking. Dazed, Kirk stared at the parking lot. Most of the water had drained off. She'd stopped them in the nick of time, before they'd done something stupid.

"We...we can go now," Tonya muttered.

"Yeah." As she pulled slowly into the street, he wondered what would have happened had they been somewhere else. Somewhere private. Somewhere appropriate for lovemaking.

He'd never know.

Except for brief directions, he didn't speak as she drove him the rest of the way home. She, too, was silent. Kirk guessed she felt awkward, but he said nothing to ease her discomfort.

When she pulled up at his apartment, he made no attempt to prolong the evening. She turned to him, her eyes full of questions.

He didn't answer them. "Thanks for the ride," he said. "I'll see you Monday."

"Monday," she echoed. "How will you get to work?"

"I'll call Ramon." He got out of the truck and watched her drive away.

It was bad enough when he only wanted her, he mused. Now he needed her. And damned if he didn't really like her, too.

Different worlds, he reminded himself as he had so many times. Black sheep or not, she was a Brewster, and he'd grown up on the streets of the inner city. If she showed up at home with him, her conservative family would be appalled. He'd done the right thing by letting her go tonight.

"The right thing," he said aloud. So why did it feel so wrong?

ON SUNDAY MORNING with the weather clear again, Tonya watched the uniformed attendant drive the pickup into the automatic car wash. Like giant jaws, the brushes separated and gulped the truck into the maw of the machine, pushing the vehicle along the belt to be scrubbed, waxed and polished until it shone. Tonya ambled beside it, watching the procedure and thinking about the afternoon she'd spent with Kirk. In fact, she'd thought of little else for two days.

What a frustrating man. Again he'd left her wanting. Of course, the parking lot had not been the time or place for lovemaking, but she'd thought surely he'd invite her up to his apartment. But no. Weren't *women* the ones who were supposed to blow hot and cold?

She knew he wanted her. She couldn't have made a mistake, not with his rock-hard erection pressing against her, not with his heart going like a trip-hammer against her breast.

And, darn it, she wanted him, too. She wouldn't have believed it could happen, but this perplexing man who'd gone from berating her to laughing with her to kissing her within an inch of her life had wormed his way into her thoughts and into her heart.

He wasn't smooth and sophisticated like most of the men she'd dated. He was gruff and tough. And he wore an air of danger as naturally as some men wore designer clothes.

After all these years of dating all the right men, she'd met Mr. Wrong. And, God help her, she was falling in love with him.

How could she get him to love her back?

She'd figured out why he disliked her being at the OK Center—he resented the power she held over them. Away from the center, when their relative positions didn't matter, the tension between them eased. Now she just had to think of a way to spend some quality time with him. Not work time, but play time.

She watched as the truck rolled off the conveyor belt and onto the asphalt. Half a dozen eager young men converged on it to spruce up the inside, provide a final shine and collect their tips.

Broad grins and enthusiastic thank-yous followed her as she got into the truck, but she paid no attention. Her eyes focused on a manila folder lying on the front seat. It hadn't been there before. The car-wash guys must have found it under the seat. The name Germain Parker was printed on the tab. Kirk had left it in the truck.

"Destiny," Tonya said with a satisfied grin. Oh yes, just when she'd been searching for an excuse to be with him, fate had played right into her hands.

Delighted, she sped toward home to change from her jeans into something sexier.

Kirk's kisses had told her a lot more than he'd intended. He might not be in love with her yet, but she'd gotten through to him every bit as much as he had to her.

"And, honey," she murmured, "I'm not through with you yet. In fact, I've just gotten started."

9

IT WAS A PERFECT SPRING Sunday. After Friday's storm, the sky had cleared to a deep sapphire blue, unmarred by a single cloud. Spring flowers sweetened the air—azalea, hawthorn and mimosa—and new leaves unfurled. Outside Kirk's open living room window a baby bird perched on a branch and fluttered its wings.

Shirtless, Kirk sprawled on the faded brown recliner that had once stood in his grandmother's home. He'd gotten up late and hadn't bothered to finish dressing. Jeans still unsnapped, he stretched out his legs and leaned back. From the stereo, an old Beatles number filled the room with music.

Spring. Sunshine. Flowers. The kind of day a man should spend with a lover...if he had a lover. Kirk didn't, hadn't been seriously involved since Amelia. That love affair had left scars far deeper than the ones on his knee.

Since then, he'd had one-night stands, even an affair or two, but no lovers. No one who'd been more than a sex partner. A few had been willing to be more, but he hadn't cared enough.

That was okay. He had no need for a relationship, especially with someone like Tonya, someone who could slice him to the bone when she left.

He willed himself to forget the woman who'd been crowding his mind, then shut his eyes and resolved to spend the day being lazy. A soft breeze caressed his cheeks, the music lulled him, and he drifted into a half dream. Despite his determination to erase her from his thoughts, Tonya's face swam before his eyes.

A knock on the door startled him awake. "Hold on," he called, fastening his jeans as he crossed to the door. He pulled it open.

"Hi," Tonya said. "I found your folder."

He blinked, reached automatically for the papers she thrust at him. Had he conjured her up out of his dream? No, she was real, and today she smelled like roses. And looked like—

Sweet God, she looked like all his fantasies come true.

She wore a jumpsuit in a rich pink, the color of the azaleas blooming outside his window. The material didn't hug her body but fell in soft pleats that touched on tantalizing secrets. The rounded neckline revealed her slender throat. Thin gold braiding led his eyes down a dangerously curved path to her waist, which was encircled with a wide gold belt. She wasn't blatantly sexy but softly suggestive. The sight was enough to make a grown man weep.

She'd tied her hair back with a pink silk scarf. He wanted to loosen it and bury his face in her sable mane. He wanted to do a good deal more. Instead, he stood and stared.

"Aren't you going to let me in?" she asked, her lips curving in amusement.

Let her in? If he did, he feared he'd never be able to get her out.

But she'd already breezed past him into the living room and was roaming around, examining his possessions. "Nice," she murmured, picking up a Native American basket. He'd bought it because it reminded him of a basket he'd made when he was a kid in one of those summer programs at the community center near his home. Now that he was the director of a similar center and could run the kind of program he wanted, he used the basket to remind him never to institute any useless programs. No dumb basket making at the OK Center.

"Nice music, too," Tonya continued, "but why are you sitting inside on such a beautiful day?"

He raised a brow. "Waiting for you."

She flashed one of her teasing smiles. "Now that I'm here, why don't we enjoy the weather?"

"Why not?" His mouth wasn't following his brain's advice. Hell with it, he decided. Why not make the most of a beautiful day in the company of a beautiful woman? Besides, if they stayed here much longer, he'd be apt to tear that outfit off her and sample the delights beneath it. "Be right back."

When he returned, he found her engrossed in the Sunday comics, but she tossed them aside and jumped up. "The Great Houston Duck Race is today. Have you ever been?" she asked.

"No, but I've heard of it. It's on Buffalo Bayou, isn't it?" When she nodded, he said, "Let's go."

On the way he asked, "Aren't you going to tell me about how you once beat out ten thousand entrants in the duck race and took home first prize?"

"Nah, this race is pure luck. But once I crewed on a racing yacht—"

"And single-handedly brought it in first."

"Nope," she said, and winked at him. "I fell overboard, they had to fish me out, and we came in dead last."

When they arrived at the starting point of the race along the banks of Buffalo Bayou, they joined a crowd of laughing entrants and spectators. The sun shone warmly, music blared from a loudspeaker, food smells wafted through the air. Grown-ups and children were loaded down with hot dogs, cotton candy, balloons...and tiny yellow plastic ducks. "No use coming and not entering the race," Tonya said, and he followed her to the booth and bought one numbered duck for each of them.

"Ladies and gentlemen, this annual event, sponsored by Delta Gamma, benefits the blind and visually handicapped of Harris County," said a voice over the loudspeaker. "Now grab your ducks and hightail it to the bridge. The Great Duck Race is about to begin."

Kirk cleared a path for them, and they took their places alongside the Sabine Bridge. "How will we keep track of our ducks?" Tonya wondered, then extracted a tube of lipstick from her purse and decorated them—hers with a chain around its neck and long pink eyelashes, Kirk's with a curly mustache. She studied her handiwork and grinned. "They probably won't show up, but who cares." She cocked her head. "We should name them."

"Donald and Daisy?"

"Too blah." She thought for a moment. "Denise and Denephew." Kirk rolled his eyes as she printed each duck's name on its back.

The starting gun went off, entrants tossed their ducks into the water, and the bayou became an ocean of yellow. "Can you see ours?" Tonya called as they pushed their way into the crowd thronging the banks of the bayou.

"Nope."

"Wait," she called, jumping up to see over a man's shoulder. "I think that's Denise."

Why pass up an opportunity to touch her? With his hands at her waist, Kirk lifted her off the ground. "Can you see her now?"

"Yes! There she is, right in the middle of that traffic jam."

"All of it looks like a traffic jam to me." He set her down but kept his hands at her waist and pulled her back against him. Her hair brushed his cheek. It felt like silk and smelled like roses. Tonya smiled at him over her shoulder, and the effect went straight to his groin. He stepped back before he became a more interesting spectacle than the ducks.

Tonya grabbed his hand and pulled him closer to the edge. "Come on, Denise," she shouted.

People who could reach them poked at their ducks, prodding them with tree branches. Kirk bent to pick up a stick. "Uh-uh," Tonya said, shaking her head. "If ours win, they have to do it fair and square."

They didn't win.

By the time the first ducks floated to the finish line, both of theirs were far back in the pack. "But wasn't it fun?" Tonya asked, her eyes alight with laughter as she bent to pick up her duck.

"Ducky." Kirk decided he hadn't spent such an entertaining afternoon in years. Maybe ever. He hated to see their time together end. "Let's go get some ice cream," he suggested, and led her to one of the refreshment booths.

They ambled along through the crowd, licking their chocolate-mint cones, and commented on the more outlandish getups they saw: a man in neon orange shorts held up by lime green suspenders; a group of teenagers with painted faces; a lady who appeared to be at least eighty, dressed in an off-the-shoulder blouse and a ruffled miniskirt.

As they turned in the direction of the truck, Tonya suddenly stopped. "There's Betsy Potter." She waved, and a freckle-faced woman with short blond hair dashed toward them.

She threw her arms around Tonya and hugged her. "Just the person I've been wanting to talk to."

"What about?" Tonya asked.

"Murder, what else?"

Tonya laughed and turned to Kirk. "So you don't get the wrong idea, Betsy owns Whodunit, a mystery bookstore."

"Yes, and Tonya and I were just about to ink a deal. She was supposed to plan some mystery weekends for me, but she backed out."

"To work at the Our Kids Center," Tonya said, and introduced Kirk.

"And I haven't forgiven you," Betsy continued. "I'd still like to work something out for those travel weekends. Why don't you stop by on Saturday?"

"I'll try."

"Added incentive. The new Nick Petrelli mystery will be out by then. I'll put a copy aside for you."

"Then I'll definitely be there," Tonya promised, and Betsy hurried back to the group she was with.

"So you're a Nick Petrelli fan," Kirk remarked as they strolled on.

"Yeah. You, too?"

He nodded.

"I've never missed one of his books, even when..."

"Even when what?" Kirk asked after her voice trailed off.

"Um, even when they first came out," she said, blushing.

Kirk wondered why she'd be embarrassed about reading mystery novels. "The new one, *The Pet Food Pirate*, is supposed to be his best," he remarked.

"Oh, it is."

Puzzled, he glanced at her. "You sound like you've already read it."

"Um, not exactly, but I'm sure it's the best," she said quickly. "But I don't want to talk about books. Kirk, I have an idea, a fabulous idea for—"

"Tonya Brewster."

She turned at the sound of a male voice. "Max!"

Kirk swung around and came face-to-face with one of the handsomest men he'd ever seen. Even another male couldn't help noticing the perfectly chiseled features, the deep-set chocolate brown eyes. He wore a silk shirt, khaki slacks that must have been tailored just for him, and Italian leather loafers. Kirk disliked him instantly.

"Where've you been hiding, babe?" he asked, running a finger down Tonya's cheek.

"I've been doing some work for my grandfather." She took a quick lick of ice cream and turned to Kirk. "Kirk, this is Maxwell Conner the Third."

He'd heard that name before. Scion of a prestigious, oil-rich family. Conner's grandfather was known for his philanthropic endeavors, and his father was a former Houston mayor. Maxwell Number Three was a wheeler-dealer and the darling of the gossip columnists. And, it seemed, a close friend of Tonya's. Well, why not? Her own family reeked of money.

Max spared Kirk a brief glance, then turned his attention to Tonya. "What kind of work?"

"The foundation's funding a center that works with inner-city kids. Kirk is the program director."

That caught Max's attention. He gave Kirk a speculative look, one male animal sizing up another. Apparently he decided Kirk was someone to be reckoned with because he backed up a step.

Smart move, Kirk thought. Maxwell might be polished and sophisticated, but he was no match for an ex-jock who'd scraped and clawed his way out of poverty. In a tussle Kirk could lick Max with one hand. The guy was soft. Although they weren't squaring off for battle, Max could undoubtedly scent a superior adversary. Kirk barely controlled a sneer.

"Listen, babe, give me a call when you decide to take a break. My boat's at the yacht club. We'll take her out."

"Sure. Give your folks my best." She accepted a kiss on the cheek, then grabbed Kirk's hand and pulled him toward the parking area.

"What's the hurry?" he asked, temper simmering. He'd almost forgotten Tonya belonged with the jet set until the meeting with Maxwell Conner the Third had hammered it home.

"I wanted to tell you my idea," she said. "Why don't I talk Betsy into sponsoring a mystery night fund-raiser for the OK Center? Black-tie, of course. We could have Houston mystery writers sign their books, have the guests solve a mystery, and we'd make megabucks for the center. Wouldn't that be fun?"

The fun in her idea escaped him. "Why not save money on a party? Just ask people to write checks."

"Party pooper. People are much more generous when they're having a good time."

Kirk grimaced. Dressing up like a penguin and parading around in some fancy ballroom wasn't his idea of a good time. If Tonya wanted to hang out with the party people, she could go with Maxwell Conner the Third. He hoped she'd forget the idea.

Apparently unaware of his mood, Tonya chattered on as they drove home. "I'll talk to Betsy next week. Let's see, who would be a good chairperson...?" Kirk tuned out the rest.

When she parked the truck in front of his apartment, he was only semisurprised that Tonya hopped out. "What do you have in the fridge?" she asked. "I'll fix dinner."

"Frozen pizza."

"Just my speed."

Kirk chuckled. He couldn't stay grouchy long around

her. After all, it wasn't her fault her family was rich as Midas.

Upstairs, he opened two beers while she put the pizza in the microwave. After they'd feasted on slices of pepperoni and mushroom, Kirk rinsed the dishes while Tonya perched on a bar stool. "Thanks for dinner," he said. "What a cook."

Her eyes teased as she slipped off the stool and went to stand beside him. "I could have done better."

"You do gourmet meals?"

"Well, not exactly. But I could've taken you out to eat."

Unable to resist, he slipped his arms around her. This was the first time he'd embraced her in friendship. He liked the feeling. She was more than just a woman he wanted in bed. She was a woman he enjoyed being around.

He laughed and rested his forehead against hers. "Tonya Brewster, what am I going to do with you?"

She gazed up at him, her eyes wide, then lifted a hand to his cheek. "Make love to me."

Stunned, he stared at her. Had she really asked him to make love to her? He wanted to, had wanted to from the first moment he'd seen her, but when she unbuttoned the top button of his shirt and whispered throatily, "Let me show you what I want," a mass of emotions surged up in his chest.

Amelia had wanted a football hero, not him. What did Tonya want? A fling with a tough guy who knew his way around the streets? An interlude while she took a break from the country club? An interesting story to tell the Maxwell Conners in her life?

Damned if he'd give her that.

No matter how much he wanted her.

Besides, he preferred to do the asking. As Ramon had pointed out, Kirk kept his relationships under tight control.

He couldn't seem to do that with Tonya. Hell, he couldn't even predict her.

He grabbed her hand as she undid his second button. "Is this what you came for?"

She looked away, then back. "I...no, not exactly...."

"Face it, babe," he sneered. "You're slumming."

Anger and frustration built as he waited for her to deny it, but she only echoed, "Slumming? What do you mean?"

"Finding out how the other half lives. Isn't that what you had in mind—a quick roll in the hay with a horse of a different color, a—"

He broke off as her hand connected with his cheek.

"You bastard!" she choked. "Is that what you think of me? Well, you can just—" He dodged her hand when it shot out again "—go...to...hell."

She spun around and dashed out of the apartment. The last thing he saw before she slammed the door in his face was her eyes, brimming with tears.

Kirk pounded his fist against the closed door. He *was* a bastard. Locked in his own anger, he'd struck out at her without a thought in his head. *He* was hurting, so he'd hurt her, too. *Good work, Butler.*

He yanked the door open and ran after her.

BLINDED BY TEARS, Tonya searched for the truck. Where had she parked the darn thing? If she didn't find it in the next ten seconds, she'd walk home. She had to get away.

She'd made an utter fool of herself. Well, she was used to that. But she'd made Kirk angry in the process. She swiped at her wet cheek. What did *he* have to be angry about?

She located the truck, stumbled over the curb, and banged her knee against the fender. Damn and double damn! She'd practically thrown herself at Kirk and he'd come back at her with that gibberish about slumming.

Oh, Lord, how was she going to face him tomorrow?

She groped for her key, stuck it in the door and was turning it when a large hand closed over her wrist.

Oh, God! Who?

Before she could scream, she was turned firmly around...and faced Kirk. "Let me go," she snarled.

"No."

She jerked her knee up, aiming for a vulnerable spot, but he held her so close she had no room to maneuver. She shoved against his chest. "I said, let...me...go."

"Damn," he muttered, "be still a minute." Struggling and cursing, he forced her arms to her sides.

She wished she had on high heels. Then she could grind one of those stilettos into his instep. Since that was impossible, she settled for glaring at him. "What do you want?"

"To talk to you."

She raised her chin and, because her head was the only part of her that she could move, turned away.

"Damn it, to apologize."

A leftover tear trickled down her cheek, and he let go of one of her hands and wiped the teardrop away with a surprisingly gentle finger.

"Don't be nice," she sniffed. "It doesn't suit you."

A wry smile softened his hard mouth. The grip on her arm loosened. "You're right, but I am sorry I hurt you."

She pondered that for a moment, not pleased with what she'd heard. "For hurting me, but not for what you said."

"It was a knee-jerk reaction."

"To what? Having a woman ask you to make love to her?"

"No." A flush spread over his cheeks. "To seeing the woman I wanted with another man."

Genuinely puzzled, Tonya stared at him. "What other man?"

"Maxwell Conner the Third."

"Maxwell Con— Max? You thought I was interested in him? Good Lord, I've known Max since I was three years old and he used to yank my ponytail."

"Yeah?" A smile spread across his face.

Anger drained as understanding dawned. He was jealous, Tonya thought. "I wouldn't make love with Max if he asked me, which he would never do. It'd be like going to bed with one of my cousins or my brother. Besides—" she chuckled "—Max is a prize jerk."

"My thoughts exactly." He stared into her eyes, his own eyes darkening. The hands on her shoulders began a rhythmic caress.

"So now that we have Max out of the way, can we talk about—"

"No," he whispered. "Don't talk." And he lowered his mouth to hers.

Warm and sweet, the kiss claimed her. His arms held her fast, pressing her against a body that was as hot as a furnace. Oh God, she'd never been held like this, wanted like this. She managed to free her arms, wrap them around him.

"Not enough," he gasped as they strained to get closer. He muttered curse words, whispered love words, then he lifted her off her feet.

She clung to him dizzily as he carried her up the stairs and into his apartment. He elbowed the door shut behind them and carried her into his bedroom. Then he stopped. "I'm not Max," he said, staring into her eyes, "or anyone like him. If you don't want this, tell me now."

Tonya put her hand on his cheek. She could feel the tension in his muscles, the heat radiating from him. "I don't want someone else," she whispered. "I want you. Only you."

"Thank God," he muttered, and laid her on his bed.

10

As KIRK SAT ON THE SIDE of the bed, Tonya felt the clutch of nerves. Now that the time had come, she had no idea what to expect. Kirk *wasn't* like Maxwell or any man she knew.

Would he be rough or gentle? Would they make love? Or war?

All she could be certain of was that they wanted each other. Shouldn't that be enough? With trembling fingers, she unbuttoned the top button of her jumpsuit.

"Don't." His voice was hoarse. He put his hand over hers and stilled her shaking fingers. "Let me."

She moved her hands and waited for him to yank the buttons apart. But he didn't. "Relax," he murmured. "We're going to take it easy. Slow and easy."

She was sure she couldn't relax; she was too keyed up. Every time she'd imagined this scene, the lovemaking had been wild and desperate. But he'd said "slow and easy." What was slow and easy to Kirk?

He bent over her and framed her face with his hands. Then he kissed her.

His lips moved over hers softly, slowly...and all her tension disappeared. Her eyes fluttered closed as the kiss went on and on. She hadn't expected such tenderness from him, such patience. This was a surprise. A wonderful surprise.

His lips journeyed across her face, still slowly, still carefully, as if he wanted to learn every angle, every hollow. She could hear his breath sigh in and out, feel it stir against her skin. Music drifted into the room, a sweet, mellow love song.

He drew the silk scarf from her hair, raking his hand through it as he did so. Then with tender care he slipped the earrings from her lobes and laid them, with the scarf, on the nightstand. He trailed his tongue across her throat, and she sighed aloud. At the sound, she heard his breathing quicken, felt his fingers tense and knew he struggled to go slow. But still he took his time.

He undressed her button by button, inch by inch, as if she were a treasure to be uncovered, one layer at a time. "Satin," he whispered. "Your skin is like satin."

"I want to see yours, too."

"You will," he murmured. "First I want to touch you."

As his hands played over her body, her blood began to simmer. Lights spun behind her eyes. His tongue circled her nipple; she gasped. His fingertips brushed over her thighs; she moaned. Now his hands hurried over her, now his kisses heated, deepened.

Oh, she needed him. Her arms were heavy, but she lifted them to twine around his neck. Her muscles were lax, but she pulled him closer. "I want you," she whispered.

"Soon. Very soon."

He rose and unbuttoned his shirt. His wide chest was sprinkled with fine black hair. He was beautiful, Tonya thought, and would have told him if she'd had any breath. But she could only moan.

He tugged off his jeans, then his briefs. She couldn't take her eyes from him. He was so incredibly male—aroused, strong, assured. And yet this overwhelmingly virile man treated her with gentleness.

He reached behind him to pull a small foil packet from the nightstand drawer. Quickly, he sheathed himself and knelt above her. Tonya opened her arms.

When he slid inside her, she was completely his.

Afterward they lay clasped in each other's arms. Lulled by the steady beat of his heart against hers, Tonya shut her eyes and dozed. She was, for the first time in her life, totally content.

KIRK WATCHED as Tonya stirred. Her eyes opened. Her gaze met his, then she smiled and brushed her hand over his cheek. That simple gesture dissolved the tension that had built while she slept. He knew he'd satisfied her sexually, but had he shown her that making love with her *meant* something?

He hadn't sought this out. In fact, he'd fought it—denied his needs and desires. But once he'd made the decision to give in to what they both wanted, everything had changed. Everything *mattered*. He had to know how she felt. "Are you okay?"

Her smile widened. "Mmm, I'm relaxed, just like you said." She cuddled closer. "And surprised."

He frowned, not sure he liked the sound of that. "In what way?"

"Making love was so beautiful. You made me feel... special."

"I wanted to make you feel special." He brushed a lock of hair from her cheek. "You are special."

"Thank you."

He wondered if no one had ever cherished her before. His arms tightened around her.

"I have a secret to tell you," she said. "Know how you reacted to Max? I felt the same way when I saw you with Karen Monroe."

"With— Are you kidding? Really?" He couldn't help grinning.

Tonya nipped his chin. "Yeah, really. But don't let it go to your head."

He chuckled and started to ease away, but she put her arms around him and held on. "Don't move yet."

"Okay." Their mouths were in just the right position for kissing, and for a while they were content with that. With soft, nibbling kisses that gradually lengthened, deepened until they were pressed tight against each other, breathing hard. "Again," she whispered.

With a groan, Kirk pulled another packet from the drawer. Sheathed, he plunged inside her, and she wrapped herself around him. As if they'd been making love forever, she matched his rhythm. Flesh rubbed against flesh, muscles bunched, legs tangled. Tonya cried out, his own hoarse cry followed.

Kirk thought he might never move again. Tonya's limp arms fell away from his back. "Tired?" he murmured.

"If the house were on fire, I'm not sure I could get up." She yawned. "But I should go." With a sigh, she sat up, then frowned. "How will you get to the center tomorrow without your bike?"

"I called Ramon yesterday. He's picking me up."

"Another reason for me to go."

He hadn't been thinking of the center when they'd begun this. He hadn't considered the implications. *Not smart, Butler.*

"You're right," he said slowly. "We should keep this separate from work."

When Tonya left, he fixed himself a Scotch and sat on the couch. On the stereo the Beatles sang "I Want You," yet the apartment seemed quiet without her. He could still smell her perfume.

The liquor burned going down. What had he gotten himself into? Had everything changed...or nothing? Tonya still held the center's purse strings; he and she still lived in different worlds. No, everything was the same...except now that he'd had a taste of Tonya, he wasn't sure he'd be able to contain his hunger for more.

TONYA INHALED DEEPLY and stroked the petals of the rose she'd brought for her desk at the OK Center. It was spring and she was in love. Really in love.

She'd had relationships before, but they'd been superficial. This one was different. It wasn't just the great sex, though, as her sore body attested, that was pretty magnificent. She loved Kirk's strength, his laughter, his compassion for the kids he worked with. He might insist he was a tough guy, but underneath she'd sensed a streak of gentleness.

She checked her watch. Darn, while she'd been daydreaming, the staff meeting had begun. She dashed down the hall and slid into her chair. Careful to avoid Kirk's eyes, she propped her chin on her hand and focused on Ramon.

"Next item," he said. "Charles McGuire, one of the assistant superintendents from the school district, called. They are definitely interested in working out a joint summer program with us, but we're running short on time. We need to come up with specifics *this week.* McGuire wants to come over Thursday. Kirk, Ladonna, can we do it?"

"Friend, if we gotta do it, consider it done," Ladonna said.

"I second that." Kirk's deep voice sent a shiver through Tonya. Just hours ago that same voice had been murmuring love words in her ear. Studiously, she made a note about the superintendent on her ever present yellow pad.

"Moving on," Ramon continued, "the police officers start their orientation here tomorrow. Kirk, that's your responsibility."

"We're ready to go."

"Good. Now—"

"Just a minute," Tonya said as an idea sprang to mind. "I know a feature writer for the Houston *Express*. Why don't I give her a call and ask her to do a story—pictures and all—on the mentoring program?" She glanced around the table, her gaze locking on Kirk's. She hoped to see approval there; instead she saw annoyance. Well, what did she expect? That a night in bed together would change his attitude toward her being here? Fat chance. She raised her chin in challenge. "What's your objection?" she asked him.

"Screwing around with a reporter takes a lot of time. Time we don't have. What's the payoff?"

Surprised he hadn't figured it out, she answered, "All the guys are from the Tanglewood area way across town. How will the captain you've been dealing with over here feel when he reads that in the paper?"

"Ah, I get it," Ramon said, smiling broadly. "It'll embarrass the sh—I mean, shoes off him."

"Right."

"Great idea, Tonya. Let's do it," Ladonna said.

Tonya glanced back at Kirk. "Sure," he said. "Go for it." But he didn't look pleased.

The heck with him, Tonya told herself.

When the meeting was over, she headed back to her office and kept busy for the rest of the morning.

In the afternoon Germain showed up. "What you want me to do?" he asked.

She'd prepared a list. "You can start in the study room. Put the books on the shelves in alphabetical order, then make a list of what we have. When you finish, bring me the list and then you can start on the windows. They need washing."

His mouth opened, then shut. "You want me to wash *all* them windows?" he croaked.

"All."

"But you got— I bet you got a hundred of 'em."

"*All*," she repeated.

He backed toward the door. "I can't do that in one afternoon."

"Right," she said, suppressing a grin. "Take as long as you need."

Grumbling, Germain left her office. An hour later, he returned with the list of books and she showed him where the cleaning supplies were. "You can start in my office," she told him.

She watched him work. He was sloppy and disorganized. Leaving a trail of soapsuds between the bucket and the window. Sloshing the sponge down one window, then moving to the next before finishing the first. He'd never be finished the way he was going about the job. "Germain," she said finally, "you need a system."

He turned to her, a puzzled frown wrinkling his brow. "What you mean, a system?"

"Squeeze out the sponge and start here." She pointed to the top of the left-hand window. "Scrub that one, then the next, then rinse them both. You'll get done faster that way."

He considered her suggestion, nodded and gave it a try. After a few minutes, he tossed down the sponge in disgust. "Dumb system's too hard."

"Oh, come on," Tonya said. "I bet you have a system in basketball."

"I don't know," he said, pondering, "but basketball's different."

"Why?"

"'Cause I like it," he answered without hesitation. He leaned against the wall. "Basketball's where it's at, you know? Guys like Jordan and Shaq and Hakeem, they got it all."

"And that's what you'd like to have."

His eyes lit up. "Yeah."

The kid had big dreams. Tonya looked at him thoughtfully. "If that's what you want, then you'd better get in all the practice you can, start getting there on time." When he started to protest, she held up a hand. "I bet Hakeem would tell you the same thing."

"Yeah, I know, but hard's I try, I can't. I don't be late on purpose, but time, it just gets away from me."

"Like your homework gets away."

He nodded glumly. Tonya smiled. She could relate to that. In fact, she could connect with a lot of what Germain said. She'd been like that at his age—still was, to a great extent.

"Maybe you could do your homework here at the center. You saw that study hall."

"I could if I'd remember what it was," Germain said. "That's the hard part."

How many times had she made the same excuse? She could have done the homework if she'd only remembered the assignment. She bet Germain didn't get any further with that reason than she had. She wished she knew how to help him. Heck, if she did, she'd help herself. Maybe the school would know a way. Karen Monroe had said something about scheduling Germain to see the counselor. It was too late today, but tomorrow she'd call and talk to the principal.

She glanced at Germain, who stared into space. "You'd better get that window washed, or you're going to be working here for a long time." He jumped up and went back to work. By the time he finished the windows in her office, Tonya decided it was time to quit. "Go put the cleaning supplies away and meet me at the front door. I'll drive you home."

She meandered down the hall, hoping to run into Kirk. But he'd made himself scarce all day. As she passed the open door of the study hall, she heard his voice. Pausing, she glanced inside. He sat across a table from Toby Carson, books spread out between them. Toby's expression was earnest, Kirk's understanding. This was not the time to interrupt. Besides, Tonya thought as she continued down the hall, this time Kirk could come to her.

TONYA DROVE GERMAIN HOME again the next afternoon. She'd spoken to Karen Monroe that morning, and the principal had suggested that Germain be tested by the diagnostician. "However," she added, "his mother will have to fill out a request, and getting her to do that may be a problem."

Karen had called back an hour later, saying that the school had an open slot for testing next week.

"If you send the papers with Germain, I'll see that they're signed," Tonya had promised. And she would, she told herself, even if she had to camp outside the boy's door.

"Here we are." Tonya pulled up before the small house where Germain lived. It was a sorry excuse for a home, with its peeling paint, sagging front porch and weed-infested yard.

As Germain opened the door of the truck, a tall, thin woman with a hairdo that resembled an untidy bird's nest came around the side of the house. "Uh-oh, there's my mama," Germain muttered.

"Germain! Where you been?" the woman shouted.

"I tol' you, I been goin' to the OK Center after school."

She peered at the truck. "What you doin' in that pickup?"

"Miss Tonya from the center, she drove me home."

His mother peered suspiciously at Tonya and scowled. "Yeah? Well, you get on in and do your homework right now, hear?"

Germain scuttled across the yard and into the house.

This was her chance, Tonya decided, and opened her door. "Mrs. Parker," she called.

The woman paused on her way to the door. "What you want?"

"I wanted to talk to you about Germain," Tonya said, coming up and extending her hand.

Mrs. Parker ignored the hand. "He in some kind of trouble?"

"No." Tonya decided to omit any mention of the broken window. "I know he has trouble at school sometimes—"

His mother sniffed. "Sometimes! You mean all the time."

"The school wants to schedule some testing. They think they can find a way to help him. If you'll just fill out these papers—"

"What for? Ain't no help for Germain. That boy's not worth spit."

Tonya gasped. How could a mother say that about her child? With an effort, she controlled her temper. "I think he's got the potential to do better, Mrs. Parker, but we all need to work together. The papers—"

"Don't have time for no papers."

"Please." Tonya grasped the woman's arm. "Don't you see? They can help so...so he won't be so much trouble to you."

Apparently that got Mrs. Parker thinking. She stared dubiously at Tonya, then said, "Give 'em here." She snatched the handful of papers and the pen Tonya hurriedly extracted from her purse. "I ain't got no faith in this school testing stuff," she muttered. But she sat on the porch steps and filled out the forms, then thrust them back into Tonya's hand. "Don't bother me no more," she said, and went inside, slamming the door.

Success! Tonya tucked the papers under her arm. *And I'll bother you again if I have to, Mrs. Parker. As much as it takes.*

"DARN IT, SAM." Two mornings later Tonya leaned an elbow on her desk and stared morosely through the window of her office as she spoke into the telephone. "Kirk Butler is the most exasperating man I've ever met."

"So blow him off," her cousin said.

"Easy for you to say," Tonya muttered, drawing a circle on her notepad. "You're not in love with him."

"And you are?"

"Yeah, I am."

Sam hesitated a moment, then said, "You've thought you were in love before."

"But never like this." She made dots for eyes and a nose and added a sad mouth inside the circle. "He's wrong for me, I know it, but—"

"Why's he wrong?"

"I could give you a list."

"Okay, start with reason number one."

"Well..." Pinned down, she found it hard to think of reasons. "He's unpredictable," she decided. "I never know what to expect from him."

"You've been known to be unpredictable," Sam pointed out. "Just a minute," she said. "Wade wants to tell me something. Yes, honey." She waited a moment, then asked, "When will you be back?" Another moment.

This time Tonya heard a soft sigh of pleasure and imagined, with envy, Wade leaning over to kiss Sam goodbye. "Shall I let you go?" she asked.

"No, we'll finish later." Sam's voice held a laugh. "Now, back to Kirk. Why don't you bring him to Granddad's birthday party Saturday evening? I'll look him over and give you my opinion."

"Good idea. If I can corner him long enough to ask."

"Go work on it," Sam suggested, and they hung up.

Should she invite him? Tonya wondered. She'd promised herself she'd wait for him to make the first move. But he hadn't. With a sigh, she ordered herself to get back to work. She needed to tell Ramon she'd spoken with her friend at the *Express*. She got up and was halfway across her office when Kirk walked in.

A glad smile sprang to her lips but she controlled it. Damned if she'd let him know how pleased she was to see him. Why had she bothered missing him, anyway?

"Hello, Kirk," she said, keeping her voice bland. "Did you want something?"

"Yeah." He reached behind him and shut the door. "You."

Before she could speak, he caught her in his arms and kissed her. Pressed against him, heart pounding, she remembered why she'd missed him. No one else had ever brought such fire, such excitement with just a touch of his lips.

He drew back and looked at her. His eyes were dark, fierce. "I tried to stay away. Damn it, I couldn't."

"I didn't want you to." One hand fisted in his hair, the other wrapped around his neck. "Kiss me again."

His kiss tasted of urgency, of desperation. He pressed her tightly against his body while his hands roamed over her, reawakening every nerve ending.

"All week I've wanted to kiss you," he muttered against her mouth, "to touch you." His hands molded her breasts, traveled along her thighs, set her on fire. She struggled with his buttons, dragged his shirt apart to expose his chest and kissed him with the same wild desperation.

He lifted her, fitting her closer against him. She wrapped her legs around him. Felt him set her on the desk. Heard a thud as her dictionary, which had been open in front of her, slid off and landed on the floor. Her hand fell to the side, and pens and paper clips flew in all directions.

"I want you. Now."

"Yes." The word trembled through her lips. She squirmed out of her jeans and panties as he fumbled in his pocket for protection. Fevered excitement tore through her. He shoved his jeans and briefs down but didn't bother to pull them off. He ripped the packet open. Then he was over her, his weight pressing her down against the cool wood of the desk. Papers scattered, her In tray crashed to the floor. She didn't care, couldn't have cared if the entire staff showed up at her door. All that mattered was Kirk and what was happening between them.

Hot sweaty bodies. His flesh against hers. His mouth. His eyes black and intent. Heavy, panting breaths as if they were running a marathon. His cry muffled against her shoulder as he reached his climax. Then her own orgasm, blinding in its intensity.

She couldn't stop trembling. Kirk raised himself off her, helped her sit up. She took a steadying breath and smiled. "Hello, did you have an appointment?"

He laughed and cupped her cheek to bring her forward for a kiss, a gentle one this time. "I had a fantasy of doing that, but on my desk."

"I don't think my heart *or* my back could take another round."

The telephone rang.

Tonya reached for it, found it teetering on the corner of the desk and hoped her voice was halfway normal. "Hello."

"McGuire's here," Ramon said.

"Wh-who?"

"From the school district. I'll be touring him around. Have you seen Kirk?"

"Y-yes." She suppressed a giggle as she glanced at the half-naked man who was struggling to pull up his jeans. *More of him than you could imagine.* "He's right here. I'll fill him in." She held out the phone for Kirk to replace. "Ramon's bringing the superintendent around. Oh, Lord." She looked at the office, at herself. "We've got to clean up."

She tugged her clothes on, dropped to her knees and swept pens and papers into an untidy pile. A bottle of toner for her printer had broken in its fall and a puddle of black liquid stained the floor. "Paper towels," she said to Kirk. "Hurry."

When he returned, she was scrambling around the floor, picking things up, dropping them and picking them up again. Kirk joined her. Together, they managed to deal with the mess on the floor and put her desk into some kind of order.

"You have paper clips in your hair," Kirk said.

She combed her fingers through her hair, sending half a dozen clips flying in all directions. How soon would Ramon and McGuire show up?

"Oh, wait! There's lipstick on your cheek." She grabbed a paper towel and scrubbed at Kirk's face.

"Ow! Leave me some skin."

She cleaned the last trace of lipstick off and tossed the towel in the trash, then dropped into her chair. Kirk took the chair across from her seconds before Ramon knocked at the door. He introduced McGuire. Tonya gave him her most dignified smile and put out a hand.

It was streaked black from the toner, and Kirk had a matching spot on his sleeve. Oh, no, she thought with horror as she jerked her hand back and muttered something about cleaning up a spill. Then the humor of the situation struck her and a laugh bubbled up. With difficulty, she suppressed it.

McGuire chatted with them for a few minutes, then Ramon ushered him out. Ramon glanced back over his shoulder as he left.

After the door closed, Tonya asked, "Think he guesses what happened here?"

"If he does, he's jealous as hell," Kirk said.

"What would McGuire think if *he* knew?" The laughter she'd stifled before spilled over. She giggled until tears ran down her cheeks. Kirk's deep chuckle echoed hers.

Finally he stood. "I'd better go before..." His hand on the doorknob, he turned. "Spend the evening with me." His grin flashed. "My bed's softer than your desk."

"It's a deal, if you'll come with me to my grandfather's on Saturday. Six o'clock. It's his birthday."

A wary look replaced his smile. "You want me to go to your grandfather's birthday party?"

"Sure. He always tells us to bring friends. You'll enjoy yourself. And you'll get to meet Sam."

"Is it...formal?"

Tonya laughed. "Of course not. Granddad hates formal. It's casual."

His mouth hardened. "What's casual in your family?"

"Top hat, white tie and tails," she snapped. "What do you think casual is? It's khakis and a sport shirt."

Relaxing visibly, he smiled. "It's a deal. I'll pick you up."

Her eyes lit up. "On your bike?" What a splash they'd make, roaring up on the Harley.

"I have a car, too."

"Oh," she said, disappointed. "I guess we'll make do."

He came around the desk and gave her a quick, hard kiss. "Yeah, we will. See you tonight."

"Okay. By the way," she added in a sultry, Mae West voice, "anytime you want to play rough again, big boy, you just let me know."

11

EVEN DRESSED CASUALLY, Tonya stood out from the crowd, Kirk thought as she settled beside him in the car on Saturday. She wore a turquoise split skirt and a hot pink, low-necked blouse. Half a dozen gold bracelets jangled on her arm, and double gold hoops gleamed at her ears.

He'd planned to pick her up at five-thirty, but she'd called in a panic at four, saying she'd forgotten to buy a gift for her grandfather. Now they sped toward the Galleria. "I'll just duck in and pick something up," she said.

"What?"

She shrugged. "I'll think of something. Did I tell you I've made arrangements for Germain to be tested?"

"No," he said, surprised. "Why?"

"Maybe he has some kind of learning problem."

"I doubt it," he said. "His problems are behavioral, pure and simple. And what can testing show? If they get him on a good day, he'll look fine. On a day when he's off the wall, the results will be different."

"I would hope a good diagnostician could see beyond that," Tonya said. "You have a one-sided view of Germain. I wish you'd try to see him differently."

"Your view is pretty biased, too. It's through rose-colored glasses."

"No, it's not." Tonya twisted her fingers in her lap. "I see him through my own experience. I was just like him at his

age—mixed-up, disorganized. My self-esteem was so low it
was nonexistent."

"Yours?" He was amazed that the woman beside him
had ever suffered from a lack of self-confidence.

"Yes, I was failing in school. Not because I couldn't do
the work, but because I didn't. I never got home with my
assignments—I always lost them on the way. My parents
were at the end of their ropes."

"How'd you get over it?"

"I didn't. I just got better, or to hear my family tell it, less
inadequate."

He heard an old despair in her voice and reached for her
hand. "Hey, you look pretty good to me."

"Thanks."

"But you can't judge Germain by your standards. You
don't have a clue what that kid's life is like."

"Don't I? I had the pleasure of meeting his mother. I
know you disagree with me, Kirk, but I feel a bond with
Germain, just like you do with Toby Carson, and I'm going
to do everything I can to help him succeed."

"I admire you for that," he told her sincerely, "but don't
be disappointed if—"

"Don't say it," she warned. "I don't want to fail."

"God knows I don't want you to, either. Just like I don't
want to fail with Toby. I've talked to your friend Rusty
about acting as his mentor."

"That's wonderful. Rusty's a great guy, very patient."
She grinned. "He has to be. He puts up with me."

They pulled into the Galleria parking garage, and Tonya
jumped out and rushed into the busy mall. "Let's try the
Texas Store first." She dashed through the store, scanning
the displays, muttering to herself. "Not here." She headed
for Macy's. "Did I tell you I talked with Betsy at Whodunit
this morning?" she asked as she maneuvered through the

mall, dodging other shoppers. "She wants me to set up a mystery weekend in El Paso. In return she'll sponsor the fund-raiser for the center. In fact, she was thrilled when I told her I could get Paul Warden to donate some signed copies of his books."

"Paul Warden, the author of the Nick Petrelli series? How can you get him? No one knows who he really is."

"I do."

Kirk waited but she said nothing. "Who is he?"

"Ah, that's a secret known only to a select few. Maybe I'll tell you...someday." She charged down the mall. "So what do you think about the fund-raiser? Great, isn't it?"

"I don't know. I—"

"Oh, look. Radio Shack. Let's go in." She dragged him inside, picked up a futuristic telephone, then an electronic organizer, and discarded them both. "Uh-uh." She hurried on to Macy's and darted inside. Pausing in the men's department, she cocked her head. "Suspenders. Or do they call them braces now? You should get some, Kirk. You'd look great." She lowered her voice. "With trousers or without."

Chuckling, he followed her as she made a foray through the department store. She dashed from counter to counter, shaking her head. Kirk felt dizzy. If the rest of Tonya's family were like her, he'd need motion sickness pills to get through an evening with them.

At last she settled on a book at Brentano's, explaining that her grandfather was a Texas history buff. She had the book wrapped, stopped to pick up a birthday card, then linked her arm with Kirk's and started back for the garage, chattering all the way to the car. The way she leapt from one topic to another, he could hardly keep up.

"Whew," he muttered when he got behind the wheel, "I'm exhausted. Do you do this often?"

"Constantly." She glanced at her watch. "We're late," she said and shrugged. "They'd faint if I showed up on time."

"Maybe you're more like Germain than I thought," he said, raising a brow.

"I am." Her voice took on a British accent. "Now, the rest of my family is veddy punctual. All my cousins are workaholics and geniuses, too, which has made them fabulously successful."

"They sound dull."

"Some of them are. Personally, I think all work and no play makes for great fortunes and tired blood."

Kirk made as good time as he could driving to Tonya's grandparents' home, but they were indeed late. Even so, when he turned into the grounds, he couldn't help but slow the car. Gardens ablaze with spring flowers surrounded the white antebellum mansion, and magnificent moss-laden oak trees shaded it. He noticed a pool, a greenhouse and another small structure that Tonya explained was a guest house. Good Lord, a guest house!

"We'll save the guest house for another visit," Tonya said and led him to the door.

It was answered by a butler—a butler, for God's sake— who showed them into a living room furnished in antiques and dominated by a marble fireplace. Kirk thought of the song, "If My Friends Could See Me Now." Yeah, if his childhood friends could imagine him in a place like this, they'd picture him climbing in a second-story window and snitching the family jewels. Nervously, he straightened his shirt. He didn't belong here. Damned if he'd let them know how he felt, though. He squared his shoulders and surveyed the room.

Beside the massive fireplace stood a gray-haired man who looked as if he might have been an NFL linebacker in his younger days. As they approached him, Kirk saw that he wasn't as large as he appeared. His bearing, not his size, was striking.

Tonya waltzed up to him and kissed his cheek. "Hello, birthday boy. Where's your party hat?"

His laugh was deep, rumbling. "Must've forgotten it."

"I brought you one." She reached in her bag and pulled out a cardboard crown with the logo of a fast-food restaurant and set it on his head at a rakish angle. Then she turned and tugged Kirk forward. "Granddad, this is Kirk Butler."

"Program director of Our Kids Center," Clint Brewster said, not at all discomfited by the ridiculous headgear. "Good to meet you. Tonya's been telling me what a good job you're doing over there. Tonya, fix Kirk a drink and introduce him around."

They headed first toward a handsome middle-aged couple standing with an older woman. "My parents and grandmother," Tonya said. "Mother and Dad are in from Moscow, where they've been teaching the Russians to love chili."

Her mother, Jeanette, was an older, more contained version of Tonya. Tall, slim, with the same wide brown eyes and glorious sable hair, she lacked Tonya's lightheartedness and her extroverted nature. In fact, she seemed a bit shy.

Kirk liked her father better. Although Roger Brewster appeared stern at first glance, Kirk sensed humor beneath the sober mien. He mentioned that to Tonya as they moved on across the room, and she laughed. "He needed a sense of humor to put up with my antics as a kid."

Kirk couldn't help but be impressed by the family's successes. Tonya's father and uncles were involved, of course, with Down Home Foods, the family business. Her grandmother and aunts, like most women of their generation, didn't work, but Kirk sensed they wielded power nonetheless.

Then there were the cousins. Claudia, who had turned a fledgling temporary employment agency into the largest concern of its kind in the South. Hal, her husband, a corporate lawyer and a partner in one of the city's biggest firms. "Successful but dull," Tonya whispered as they moved on to another group.

She introduced him to Sam's younger sister Susan next. Quiet and unassuming, she was a dress designer who was making a name for herself not just nationally, but internationally. And to Stuart, the banker, former wannabe race car driver. Kirk met Ryan, Tonya's brother, possessed of the same mischievous grin as his sister. And, finally, Sam, who, with her husband, owned a large private detective agency, now known as a security firm.

Meeting Tonya's family in person after hearing her describe them gave him plenty to think about. For some reason, this woman with impressive attributes of her own didn't feel she measured up. Hard to believe, after the way she'd barreled into the OK Center. For the first time, his resentment at her position there diminished. Instead, he felt a strong desire to protect her, care for her. Not that she'd want to hear his feelings. Extend a helping hand to Tonya and she'd be likely to bite it off.

Sam interrupted his reverie. "Come and sit down."

He sat beside her on a dainty, damask-covered love seat that made him feel big and out of place. But Sam, he discovered quickly, had a knack for making people comfortable. "Tonya tells me you're the center's official jock."

"I coach whatever sport's in season. Right now it's basketball."

"I'm a fan," Sam told him. "Wade and I have season tickets to the Rockets games." Her eyes gleamed with mischief. "I like speed."

"So does your cousin," Kirk said with a dry smile.

"You've driven with her," Sam concluded. When he nodded, she chuckled. "It's an experience."

"No kidding. She almost sank us during the flood last week. But I probably shouldn't have told you that. She was driving your husband's truck."

Sam laughed. "If he let Tonya use it, he knew he was putting the poor vehicle's life on the line."

Kirk leaned back and studied Sam thoughtfully. "Tonya likes speed. You must go for danger."

"Why do you say that?"

He smiled at her. "Private investigating isn't a typical career choice for...young ladies."

Sam burst out laughing. "Exactly what my mother told me. But it's not the danger that attracts me. It's the challenge."

"I think you and Tonya are alike," he said.

Sam nodded, her expression serious now. "Tonya needs to watch herself. Sometimes she takes on too big a challenge."

There was a message here, but whether the too big challenge was the OK Center or him, Kirk wasn't sure, and Sam didn't seem inclined to say more.

"I'm sorry you won't get to meet Wade this evening," she said. "He's in Dallas on business until tomorrow. By the way, he knows some people in the Rockets' organization. If you're interested in having someone speak to your basketball players, let us know."

That could be the key to Toby Carson...and maybe to Germain, too, he thought excitedly. "Thanks, I will."

After their brief conversation, he decided that of all the Brewsters, Sam impressed him most. Regal and beautiful, but with a wild streak below the surface. She was quite a woman.

Later Tonya's grandfather invited Kirk to look over a collection of Texas memorabilia housed in the study. An excuse to get him away for a private talk, Kirk was sure.

The study was small but impressive, with bookshelves housing volumes on Texas history and glass cases containing artifacts from the state's early days. Clint showed Kirk his collection, then gestured to one of two armchairs in front of a small fireplace.

Clint asked general questions about the center as befitted a social occasion. "I'm glad to help you out," he said. "I grew up in a rough area, too—around the oil fields—so I know that kind of life. I'm a tough old coot myself."

That surprised Kirk. Maybe he'd heard somewhere that Clint came from a modest background, but he hadn't absorbed the information. In his mind, rich people had always had money. Hearing Clint Brewster talk about his roots gave him something to mull over.

"You need to come by one day and see what we're doing," Kirk said. "Especially to see what your granddaughter's done. She's contributed a lot."

"Tell me more about that," Clint said.

As he listed Tonya's accomplishments, he realized he wasn't exaggerating for her grandfather's benefit; he meant it. "She's enthusiastic and creative," he said, "and those qualities make a difference in a facility like ours."

Clint nodded. "I imagine the OK Center has contributed as much to Tonya as she has to you."

"What do you mean?" Kirk asked.

"You've given her a mission. Everyone needs one. Now Sam—hers is to save the world. Tonya wants to save the little piece of it around the OK Center." Shrewd blue eyes assessed Kirk. "Your mission's the same, I reckon."

"Yes, sir."

"Not a bad goal for either one of you." He rose. "Let's go back and join the crowd."

When they returned to the living room, Kirk excused himself and went to look for a bathroom. The closest one was occupied, so he wandered down to a bedroom and into the bathroom next door to it.

Man, the bathroom was opulent. A sunken tub with a whirlpool and gold faucets. Miniature bottles of perfume. Bars of soap in the shape of dolphins and swans. Even a bidet. He thought of the one and only bathroom at his grandmother's house. Heck, she wouldn't know what a bidet was for. He wasn't absolutely certain himself. What the heck was he doing here in this enclave of privilege? He didn't belong here any more than Tonya did on Magnolia Street. Yet he couldn't make himself stay away from her.

He washed and dried his hands, feeling uncomfortable leaving the fancy satin-appliquéd towel damp, then wandered back toward the living room. The bell rang as he neared the hallway, and he saw the butler open the door for a tall, broad-shouldered man with dark, wavy hair and striking blue eyes.

Footsteps sounded, and Kirk turned to see Sam dash to the door and hurl herself into the man's arms. "Wade! You're a day early," she said, looking up at him with such adoration that Kirk's heart contracted.

"Couldn't sleep without you," Wade said, and kissed her as if he'd never let her go. Kirk stayed in the shadows, feeling like a voyeur but unwilling to interrupt their reunion. Wade drew back to look at Sam. His hands traveled over her face, then he reached behind her, freed her long blond hair from the clip that held it and buried his face in it. "Can we go home?" he asked.

She put her arm around his waist and urged him toward the living room. "After dinner."

"Eat fast."

Kirk waited a few minutes, then strolled back to the living room. Tonya saw him and jumped up. "Come and meet Wade."

The two shook hands. Kirk knew Wade Phillips was sizing him up. He didn't mind; he was doing the same. He decided he liked the man.

"Kirk Butler," Wade said slowly. "Tonya mentioned your name, but until I saw your face, I didn't make the connection. You played in the NFL a while back, didn't you?"

Kirk nodded. Recalling his football days wasn't one of his favorite pastimes. "Yeah, I had a short career."

"I remember. Tough way to end it."

"It ended at the beginning," Kirk said, feeling the expected pang. He noticed that Tonya was listening intently, her brow furrowed. She said nothing, though, and he was relieved.

"So now you're doing some good for kids," Wade said. "I admire that."

"Someone has to help these kids. I imagine, in your business, you see a lot of the same things I do," Kirk said.

"Yeah, both Sam and I see the raunchy side of life." He patted Sam's knee. "I tried to get her to stay out of it, but she's one stubborn woman, aren't you, darlin'?"

"You better believe it," Sam said.

"It's a family trait," Tonya added, "but you already know that, don't you, Kirk?"

Man, did he ever.

"Dinner is served," the butler announced from the doorway.

Tonya slipped her hand in Kirk's as they headed for the

dining room. "Will you come home with me after dinner?" she asked softly.

Kirk nodded. Thinking of the night to come made his pulse accelerate. Silently, he echoed Wade's request: *Eat fast.*

12

LATER THAT EVENING, Tonya threw open the door to her town house and flipped on the light. "Welcome to the world of Tonya Brewster."

Had he expected interior design perfection in this home? Brewster family sophistication? Knowing the inhabitant as well as he did by now, he shouldn't have. This dwelling had a haphazard, "Tonya" look. Contemporary funk.

A roomy couch upholstered in off-white sat in the center of the room. Pillows in contrasting and sometimes clashing colors were piled over it helter-skelter. A one-eyed stuffed hippo in hot pink stared solemnly at him from the far end of the sofa. The coffee table boasted a pair of expensive-looking crystal birds, an art book from the Metropolitan Museum of Art and a garish plastic Donald Duck with Disney World stenciled on its back. On the floor beneath the coffee table, a lone sandal lay on its side beside a rubber mouse.

Tonya watched him look around. "This place won't make *Better Homes & Gardens*," she said.

"No, but it's you."

"Come and sit down," she said, patting the couch, "and I'll introduce you to— Oh, there you are." A long-haired gray tabby kitten skittered across the room and jumped into her lap. Tonya held him up and rubbed her forehead against his. "This is Butler."

Kirk raised a brow. "Named after your grandfather's butler?"

"After you. He moved in the week I met you."

Kirk threw back his head and laughed, then pulled Tonya into his lap and hugged her. "If I'd known you were thinking about me, I wouldn't have waited so long."

"To what?"

"To kiss you."

"You didn't...wait long, I mean. Wanna do it again?"

"Mmm-hmm." He was already unbuttoning her blouse, already pulling it from her shoulders. Her skin was so soft. He buried his face between her breasts. "You smell like musk tonight," he murmured. "Another surprise."

"I'm just full of them," she said between kisses, then unfastened his shirt.

He shrugged it off along with the rest of his clothes and kissed her again. He helped her undress and they cuddled together, kissing, touching. Here on the couch, with Tonya in his arms, surrounded by colorful pillows and the hippo glowering at him with its one eye, he felt happier than he could ever remember. He kissed Tonya's shoulder and—

"Ow!"

"What's wrong?"

"There are three of us here, and one is a cat. With claws."

"Let's see." They sat up and she examined his back. "Poor baby, he really got you. Come in the bedroom, and I'll make it better. Oh, and bring one of those little foil jobs...just in case."

"Not 'in case.' For sure." He slipped the packet out of his pants and followed her into her room.

"*You* stay out," she ordered, shaking her finger at the kitten as she shut the door. She pulled a patchwork quilt off the bed, tossed it into the corner and patted the bed. "Lie down. I'll be right back."

He lay on his stomach and closed his eyes. In a minute, he heard her return and felt something cold on his back, then the sting and odor of alcohol. "Jeez."

"It's just alcohol. Don't be a baby." Next she rubbed on something creamy, and the sting went away. "Want a massage?" she asked.

"If you're using alcohol, no thanks."

Her voice lowered to a seductive purr. "Musk oil." She climbed onto the bed and straddled him. Something warm trickled down his spine, and she began to smooth it over his back. "Feel good?"

"Mmm."

"Just relax."

Her hands were like magic. She worked every muscle from his shoulders to the soles of his feet. Interspersed with the ministrations of her hands were the soft kisses she planted over him. Her breath tickled along his spine, his buttocks, the backs of his knees. She sighed with pleasure, telling him how beautiful his body was, how strong, how perfect. He floated in a sensual haze. No one had ever cared for him like this.

"Turn over."

He obeyed, then, aroused and needy, he reached for her.

"Not yet. I'm not nearly finished with you." Then she worked the same magic on his chest, his belly, his thighs. For the first time in his life, a woman had him completely in her power, reduced to panting breaths and moans of pleasure and longing. He thought dreamily that there was something to be said for occasionally relinquishing control.

At last, when he was certain he would explode, she took the condom from his hand and fitted it on him herself, then slid over his slickened body and took him inside her. She set the pace—slowly at first, lifting and lowering so his shaft slipped in and out, then faster, riding him hard, until they both exploded. Through half-closed eyes, he saw her rear back, her expression triumphant. Then she collapsed on his chest, and they lay spent in each other's arms.

After a long time, she eased away and sat on the edge of the bed. Her eyes found the scar on his knee, and she traced it with gentle fingers. "Tell me about it."

"It's a long story."

"I've got all night." She propped a pillow against the headboard and sat, hugging her knees.

Kirk sat up, too. He might as well tell her everything. Or almost everything. "You know where I grew up. Right around the corner from the OK Center. My dad walked out when I was eight. Which was okay, because he spent most of his time drinking beer, watching wrestling on TV and griping about his sorry lot in life. Mom got a job as a waitress in an all-night café, and I stayed with my grandmother after school. She was great." He smiled, remembering. "She'd help me with my homework, play Monopoly with me, bake gingerbread cookies. Those were the best years of my childhood."

"And then?"

"Gram died when I was twelve." He still hurt, remembering how quickly she'd gone, how devastated he'd been. Tonya must have sensed that because she reached for his hand and squeezed.

"After that I pretty much took care of myself. I wasn't the best baby-sitter. I was angry at Gram for dying, angry at my mom for never being around. I started skipping school, hanging around the neighborhood. I was big for my age, and I attracted the attention of some of the tougher teenagers. They introduced me to all sorts of mischief—petty thievery, vandalism—and I was a fast learner."

Beside him, Tonya shivered, and he glanced at her. "Not a pretty story, huh?"

"Not so far," she admitted.

"You want the rest?"

She lifted his hand to her lips and kissed his knuckles. "Go on."

"I started with shoplifting. It was so easy, I couldn't believe it. No one ever noticed. I didn't take anything big, but I got a high out of it nevertheless. Then I graduated to bigger stuff. Burglary."

He waited for a reaction, but although her eyes widened, Tonya said nothing, just continued holding his hand.

"The first house was a breeze, just like the shoplifting. I got away with a TV set and three radios. I figured I was on my way to cashing in. The second time wasn't so easy. I got caught."

Her hand tightened on his. "What happened?"

"I was damn lucky. The judge ordered me into a program for nonviolent juvenile offenders. It was a mentoring program like the one we're starting. My mentor was a retired football player named Brad Mercer. He took a real interest in me and introduced me to the coach at my school. After that, I was too busy with sports to go in for crime. When I got a football scholarship to the University of Texas, Brad gave me a silver belt buckle."

"The one you always wear."

"Yeah," he said, "it's my...talisman. Brad died of cancer my sophomore year. That hurt almost as much as the death of my grandmother. Brad was more than a mentor. He was a surrogate father, and I was a kid who badly needed one.

"Anyway," Kirk went on, "I was good at football. Good enough to get a contract with the Philadelphia Eagles." He grinned at Tonya's amazed look. "It wasn't for twenty million, but it paid a nice salary. Unfortunately, my career didn't last long. One game."

She scooted down the bed and bent over to kiss the scar. "I'm sorry. What happened?"

"Two linebackers came down on me—six hundred pounds of muscle. My knee was crushed. I felt pretty lousy, but at least the Eagles owed me my salary for the year. I came back to Houston and spent a year working at dead-end jobs while I recuperated. Then I went to law school."

"You're a lawyer?"

"So my diploma says."

"But—"

"I worked in the D.A.'s office, prosecuting some of the same guys I used to hang out with, but I didn't like it. I wanted to prevent crime, not deal with it after the fact. I ran into Ramon. We'd played football together in high school, and he'd become friends with Ladonna while working in a neighborhood association. We started talking about what we could do for the kids in our old community. Our Kids is the result."

Tonya squeezed his hand. "How can you say that's not a pretty story?"

"It's not."

"You didn't turn out like Rick, did you?" she said. "I think what you've accomplished is wonderful."

"Thanks, but my story's about as far away from the Brewster saga as you can get."

Tonya grasped his chin and pulled him around to face her. "Don't say that. Don't ever say that. It doesn't matter. You and I—that's what matters." She pulled him closer and kissed him hard.

His arms wrapped around her, and he kissed her back. *You and I.* He'd like to believe that. He'd like to think the differences between them didn't matter. That would be like a fairy tale in reverse—Cinderfella ending up with Princess Charming. Yeah, that would be great, but he didn't put much stock in fairy tales. He'd learned not to believe in them a long time ago.

FIRST THING Monday morning Tonya called Sam.

"So, what did you think of Kirk?" Tonya realized she was holding the phone in a white-knuckle grip and consciously relaxed her hand while she waited for her cousin's pronouncement. She'd always respected Sam's opinion. This time especially, she wanted it to be favorable.

"Mmm," Sam said.

"That's all you have to say? 'Mmm?' Is it a good mmm or a bad one?"

"Definitely good."

Tonya let out a breath. "You liked him. You don't think he's wrong for me?"

"He's perfect for you," Sam insisted. "The three important qualities are there—he's solid, strong, and definitely sexy. What more could you ask?"

Tonya beamed at the phone. "Nothing. I just wanted someone to confirm my opinion."

"And if I didn't, would it have made any difference?"

A laugh bubbled out. "Nope, not a bit." She and Sam talked for a few minutes more and hung up.

As soon as Tonya put the phone down, it rang again. "Ms. Brewster, this is Karen Monroe."

The two women exchanged pleasantries, then Karen said, "Germain's test results are back, and everything points to his having an attention deficit hyperactivity disorder."

"I...I've heard that term," Tonya said, frowning at the phone, "but I don't really understand it."

"It means that Germain's problems in school and probably his behavior problems, too, stem from an inability to sustain attention. His mind can't stay focused, so he switches attention from one thing to another and misses things, like homework assignments. And his body can't stay in one spot, either."

"That means he has a physical problem. He's not just a bad kid, right?"

"Exactly," Karen said.

"Can it be cured?"

"That's the bad news. We can work with it, work around it, but we can't make it go away. But this is only a preliminary diagnosis. We'd like Dr. Matthew Goldsmith, the psychiatrist who consults with the school district, to confirm it and also to determine whether medication will help control it."

"Uh-oh."

"Uh-oh is right. That means we need permission." She cleared her throat. "You got Germain's mother to agree to the testing. Want to try again?"

"Sure, I'll be by to pick up the papers as soon as our staff meeting is over." She hung up and hurried to the meeting. As usual, she was late, but today at least she had a good reason.

"Well, Tonya, your idea about the feature worked," Ramon said. "We just got a call from the reluctant—the *formerly* reluctant—Captain Morales of the Magnolia police station. He practically begged me to include his officers in our mentoring program."

Lusty cheers sounded around the table, and Tonya beamed. Even Kirk seemed pleased. God, it felt good to have her accomplishments lauded. And she'd have another one to brag about if she was successful with Germain's mother.

She stopped Kirk on the way out of the meeting. "I have to run an errand. I'd like to talk to you when I get back."

"Sure." He lowered his voice. "My desk or yours?"

Tonya felt her cheeks flush and figured they were probably the same shade as her Jaguar. "Why don't we meet in the conference room?" she asked sweetly.

"Good idea. There's a long table. We can...spread out."

"Rat," she said out of the corner of her mouth, and hurried off.

She picked up the forms at Germain's school, then headed for his house.

She pulled up in front and got out of the car. A movement at the living room window indicated that Mrs. Parker was home, but no one answered her knock. She knocked again, louder. Still no response. Well, she'd just stay until the woman decided to show herself. She flopped down on the porch steps.

She waited less than ten minutes before the door opened. "What you want?" Germain's mother asked.

"To talk to you." Tonya jumped up and stood in the doorway. "I have some more papers for you to sign."

"I ain't signin' no more papers." She backed up and reached for the door.

Tonya anticipated her move and pushed the door back before the woman could slam it in her face. "At least listen. Please."

"Okay, I'm listening," Mrs. Parker said sourly.

"The school thinks Germain has a problem."

His mother let out a cackling laugh. "Right, I coulda tol' 'em that."

"It's the kind of problem they can help. They want him to see a doctor to be sure."

"What a doctor gonna do? Give him some pills? He can get pills on the street."

Tonya's patience ebbed. "Look, this might be Germain's only chance and you're tossing it away. Mrs. Parker, if you'll just sign these papers, the doctor will see Germain and—"

"How much it gonna cost me?"

"Nothing. Not one penny."

The woman stared at her suspiciously. "The school gonna pay?"

No use going into an explanation of Dr. Goldsmith's relationship with the district. "Yes."

"Well, I guess one more paper's not gonna matter. Give it here."

Tonya handed it over. She watched the woman scrawl her signature on the sheet. "Thank you, Mrs. Parker. You'll be glad you did this." She hurried away before Mrs. Parker could change her mind.

As soon as she returned to the OK Center, Tonya went in search of Kirk. She found him in his office poring over a folder on his desk. He looked up when she entered and his lips quirked with that sexy grin she loved. Mischief filled his eyes. "Are we gonna have that meeting now?"

She shut the door behind her and advanced toward him. Inches from his chair, she stopped. "Nope, later. Now I have something to tell you." Before he could grab her, she sat down. "It's good news."

She explained what the school district had determined through Germain's testing. "So he *isn't* just a bad kid. Oh, Kirk, I think there's hope for him."

"You've done a lot with him," Kirk said, admiration in his eyes. "I wrote the kid off, but you believed in him. I have to congratulate you."

"Thanks." Tonya reveled in the rare words of praise. "I can't wait until the doctor sees him and we really know. I—"

The door crashed open.

Panting, Ladonna rushed in. "Kirk, we have a problem. Hurry!"

He was already on his feet. "Where?"

"In childbirth class. Rick Henderson's back."

13

"STAY HERE!" KIRK CALLED over his shoulder as he ran out of his office. To his annoyance, Tonya paid no attention. She was at his heels all the way to the classroom.

He found Janene huddled on a beanbag chair, her face in her hands. Tears streamed through her fingers. Corelle bent over her, smoothing her hair, trying to calm her. A circle of teenage mothers-to-be surrounded her. Rick was nowhere in sight. "Where is he?" Kirk asked.

"He took off soon as Ladonna ran to get you," Corelle sniffed.

"Get rid of the spectators," Kirk said to Ladonna. He crouched beside Janene. "You okay, honey?"

She peered up at him and shook her head. "He hit me."

Sure enough, her lip was cut and swollen, her cheek sported a bruise that was already turning purple, and one eye was half-shut. "As long as you're here, get some ice for her eye," he snapped at Tonya. "Then let the cops know Rick's in the area."

"N-nooo," Janene wailed. "If Rick finds out, he'll hit me again."

"No, he won't. I promise you that." He tamped down his anger and gentled his voice. "Tell me what happened."

"I...I saw him at school yesterday. He came in the building."

And no one picked him up. Great security, Kirk thought with disgust.

"And he came over to my locker and talked to me. He said I could be his girlfriend again. H-he even gave me a ring." She held up her hand, showed Kirk a cheap gold band.

Probably stole it. And she thought that meant everything was going to be just peachy. Naive kid. "And?"

"And he met me after school today. We started walking home, but when we got near here and he saw I was goin' in, well, he got mad. I told you before he doesn't like me comin' around here."

"He got mad and punched you."

"Here's the ice." Tonya bent and placed a plastic bag against Janene's cheek. "I've called the police."

"Good. Now go call Janene's mother."

"My mother?" the girl wailed. "Why's she have to know?"

"Honey, you can't keep it from her," Kirk said. "All she has to do is look at your face and she'll know. Now, you rest here a few minutes. When your mom gets here, I want to talk to her. In the meantime," he said, grasping Tonya's arm, "I want to talk to *you.*" Ignoring the indignant look on her face, he propelled her down the hall and into an empty office.

Tonya turned on him and gritted her teeth. "What are you doing—impersonating a Neanderthal? Why didn't you just drag me in here by the hair?"

"I'm sorry. But I told you to keep out of the way."

"Don't give me orders. And stop behaving like Rick."

Damn, Kirk realized, he *was* acting like that punk. He put his hands on Tonya's shoulders and tried to keep his grip gentle, even though his temper smoldered. "I don't want you getting mixed up in a situation where you might get hurt. What if Rick had stayed?"

Predictably, her chin went up. "I would have defended myself."

"Yeah, that chin could knock him dead." A sharp longing to plant a kiss right on the edge of her pugnacious chin rushed through him, but he ignored it. "Come on, baby, simmer down."

"*Baby?*"

"Tonya. Ms. Brewster. We don't have time to argue now. I just want you to be careful."

"I know enough not to get hurt," she retorted. "And don't give me a lecture about going home where I belong. Now, I'm going to take Janene to my office while you and Ladonna talk to her mother."

"Okay." He gave in, but not too gracefully, and watched Tonya stalk out of the room.

When he returned to the classroom, Mary Lou North was already there, looking pale and shaken. "Janene, I've told you a hundred times to lose that boy. Now look what he's gone and done. You're lucky he didn't punch you in the belly."

Kirk agreed. "That's what I want to discuss with you, Mary Lou. Ms. Brewster will take care of Janene while we talk." He gestured to Tonya, and she put an arm around Janene and led the girl out.

"Let's go to my office," Kirk suggested, and signaled to Ladonna to accompany them. Once they were seated, he began. "Rick's apparently not going away. And, as you said, next time he may not stop with her—he may harm the baby."

"That no-good kid ought to be behind bars," Mary Lou said.

"We can't count on that happening in time," Kirk said. "We have to concentrate on keeping Janene out of his way.

Is there anyone she could stay with—friends or relatives in another neighborhood?''

"You...you mean, send her away?"

"For her own protection," Ladonna said.

"Th-there's no one," Mary Lou said, "leastways not in Houston."

"Somewhere else?"

"I got a sister in Lubbock."

"Can you call her?" Ladonna asked.

"I...guess so. I think she'd be willing to help me out. Yes, I can call."

"Is Janene planning to keep the baby?" Ladonna asked.

"She hasn't come to no decision on that. We've talked but she keeps changing her mind. She's still got three months."

"Whatever she decides to do, for now she needs to leave."

"You're right. I shoulda thought of it myself, but I kept hopin' Rick would stay gone."

"You'd better make the arrangements and get her out of town as soon as possible," Kirk said, and the woman nodded. "I think we should call Janene in and tell her what we've been talking about," he suggested.

He went to Tonya's office, where he found the two of them waiting. "Would you both join us," he said, deliberately including Tonya. Her eyes met his, and she smiled. He was relieved at that. He didn't like being at odds with her.

As soon as he explained the plan to Janene, he found himself at odds with *her*. The girl burst into tears. "But I'll have to leave all my friends. And Lubbock is hicksville. I won't know anybody there."

"Janene," her mother said sharply. "What you need to be thinkin' about now is your baby. You don't want Rick to hurt it, do you?'' Turning to Kirk, she muttered, ''That girl don't ever think of nobody but herself.''

''No—o, I don't want anything to happen to the baby,'' Janene said, ''but—''

''Then you'll go, and no buts. I'll call Aunt Dee tonight.''

''All right,'' the girl said, looking sullen.

Promising to call Kirk as soon as definite plans were made, Mrs. North led her daughter out. Ladonna went to the day-care room, and Kirk was left alone with Tonya.

''That was a good plan,'' she said as they walked to the door of his office.

''I thought so. Still mad at me?''

''Not so much. Maybe a little.''

He couldn't control a smile. ''If we were somewhere else, I'd kiss that pout off your lips.''

''I'll save it,'' she offered, ''and you can kiss it later.''

''Deal.'' He leaned against the door frame and watched her walk back to her office. He was enjoying the sway of her hips when Ladonna tapped him on the arm. He hadn't even realized she'd come back.

''You got it bad, friend,'' she observed.

''What do you mean?''

Her rich laugh rolled through the hallway. ''You *know* what I mean. You sleeping with her?''

For once, Kirk was speechless. ''I...''

''Yeah, you are.''

Kirk grimaced and ran his fingers through his already disheveled hair. ''I'm crazy about her.''

''And that's bad?'' she asked.

''We're different,'' he said glumly.

''Yeah, you're a male, she's a female. Sounds okay to me.''

''Hell, Ladonna, we're from different worlds. I'm from

one side of the tracks, she's from the other. You should've seen her grandfather's house."

"And you can't jump over those tracks? Friend, that doesn't sound like you. Besides, if she took you to her granddaddy's, she must think you're okay."

"I went for a visit. I wouldn't fit in on a long-term basis." Before Ladonna could protest, he went on. "Those people and us—we don't even have the same expectations." He spread his hands, trying to explain. "They live in a world of unlimited possibilities. Here, we're just trying to survive. And Tonya doesn't fit in here, either."

"Seems like she's doin' pretty well."

"What about the jacket? What about getting mixed up with Germain Parker and ending up with a broken window?"

"Okay," Ladonna conceded, "she's made a few mistakes. She's learning."

Kirk rubbed at the muscles that suddenly tightened in his neck. "We don't have the luxury of waiting for someone to learn, especially someone who's holding the purse strings." He went back to his desk and lowered himself into the chair.

Ladonna followed him into his office and took a chair across from him. "Is that what's bugging you? That she controls the money?"

"It doesn't help," Kirk admitted.

"I wouldn't sweat it," Ladonna said. "She's not gonna be doin' that forever. Six months, they said. We're almost through month number one."

"That doesn't help, either." Automatically, his fingers traveled to his belt buckle. What bothered him most about the whole situation was that in a few months, Tonya would be gone.

"You don't want her here, you don't want her gone."

He smiled ruefully. "Confusing, isn't it?"

Ladonna nodded. "Maybe you need to decide exactly what you do want."

That, Kirk thought, was easier said than done.

THE NEXT DAY TONYA SAT at her desk, staring out the window. Spring had never been so beautiful, she thought. The last remnants of winter had faded. The air was fragrant with flowers, the grass was growing, and the weather had warmed. Tonya's heart seemed full to bursting. Not just from the beauty of the season but because, for the first time in her life, she was truly in love. She had only to hear Kirk's voice, sense his presence in a room, and her heart danced.

Yesterday they'd quickly cleared up their misunderstanding about her rushing after him to check on Janene. Except for that, the misgivings he had about her being at the OK Center seemed to be diminishing, and they'd settled into a smooth routine at work. Although the center staff was mindful of Rick's presence in the neighborhood, there had been no further incidents. Janene was leaving next week for Lubbock and she had accepted, albeit grudgingly, the plans for the remainder of her pregnancy. And Germain had paid off his debt to Tonya and continued to attend basketball practice. He had not created another disturbance; in fact, he was so enthralled with the idea of Dr. Goldsmith's being able to help him that his behavior was nearly perfect. The conference to discuss his test results was scheduled in a couple of weeks, and Tonya was hopeful that a better future awaited the boy.

So work was good. And after working hours...

She and Kirk spent every night together, at his place or hers, sharing, laughing, making love. She'd begun to have hopes for the future, for something permanent between them.

"Stop daydreaming," she ordered herself. This afternoon she had work to finish. Tonight she and Kirk were—

Noises in the hallway caught her attention. Something was wrong.

She jumped up and ran out. Several of the staff crowded around someone she couldn't see. Tonya pushed through the group...and saw Ladonna leaning against the wall. Her blouse was ripped, one shoe and an earring were missing. Her hair was disheveled.

"What happened?" Tonya cried.

"Rick Henderson got hold of her," someone answered.

"She's damn lucky he didn't shoot her full of holes," commented another staff member, and Tonya cringed.

Ramon elbowed his way through the crowd. "Give her some space," he ordered. "Tell me about it," he said to Ladonna.

She let out a shaky breath. "I was walkin' back from lunch. All of a sudden someone grabbed me from behind. Yanked me by the hair," she said, trying to pat her hair into place. "I got a couple of kicks in, but then I saw who it was and I figured, Don't fight him, Ladonna, or you could end up on a slab." She shivered and hugged herself.

"Somebody get her a chair," Ramon ordered, and Corelle dragged a child-sized chair out of the day-care room.

Ladonna sat down heavily. "He told me he didn't want Janene comin' over here, and if we didn't stop nosing around in her business and his, he was gonna come after us. I believe it, too. He wasn't playing around. That threat's for real." She glanced at Kirk, who had just appeared. "You better call the police."

"I will," Kirk said, "right now. Meanwhile, all of you take this seriously. I don't want anyone out alone in the neighborhood, hear?"

The group scattered, some of the women glancing nervously over their shoulders as if expecting Rick and the Sabers to leap out of a closet.

"You did hear that, didn't you?" Kirk murmured as he passed Tonya.

She heard and heeded his warning. After all, the idea of meeting Rick or his cronies face-to-face was not appealing. Complying with Kirk's directive was easy. They came to work together and went home together, so she didn't even have to go back and forth to the parking lot alone. And she rarely had time to go out for lunch. Inside the walls of the OK Center, she felt safe.

And outside, a police officer kept watch...at first.

The rest of the staff were careful, too...at first.

But as time passed and Rick didn't make good on his threats, everyone relaxed. Staff members began frequenting the neighborhood cafés again, began exiting the center singly instead of in pairs or groups.

Within a couple of weeks, everything was back to normal.

TONYA FELT NO NEED for protection on the day of Germain's conference. She didn't even bother telling Kirk where she was going. She backed the truck out of the parking lot and, humming to herself, drove to Franklin D. Roosevelt Middle School. She glanced at her watch as she hurried into the office. Late, as usual.

The conference table was crowded. Karen Monroe sat at one end, Mrs. Parker, dressed up this afternoon in a pink rayon dress that had seen better days, sat at the other, cracking a wad of chewing gum. To provide support, Tonya took a chair beside Mrs. Parker.

The door opened, and a woman—the diagnostician, Tonya supposed—came in with Germain. He stopped at the doorway, hunched his shoulders and glanced furtively around the table. His eyes met Tonya's, and he shuffled over and took the empty seat on her other side. She gave him an encouraging nod, but he barely looked at her. He stared at his hands, which were clenched in his lap.

"Now that we're all here—" Karen began the meeting by introducing everyone—Germain's homeroom teacher, his language arts teacher, the diagnostician, the counselor, the speech clinician and Dr. Goldsmith. Tonya hoped Mrs. Parker was as impressed as she was by the number of people assembled to discuss one young boy.

The diagnostician explained the test results. Although she spoke directly to Mrs. Parker, the woman seemed uninterested. Tonya supposed Germain had come by his problem legitimately; his mother didn't attend any better than he did. Instead, she studied an obscenely long pink fingernail as if nothing happening in the room had any relation to her. Tonya was tempted to kick her under the table.

Germain shot a sidelong glance at his mother, then looked away. Tonya sensed the tension vibrating from the youngster. His jaw tightened, he clenched and unclenched his hands under the table. Finally, apparently unable to endure his mother's indifference, he leaned across Tonya. "Mama, you listening?" His stage whisper had every head turning toward him.

Every head except his mother's.

Tonya couldn't contain her disgust with Mrs. Parker a moment longer. "*Are* you listening?" she repeated, her angry whisper louder than Germain's.

Mrs. Parker cracked her gum. "I'm listening. What else you think I come for?"

Tonya tried to give Mrs. Parker the benefit of the doubt. Maybe the woman was overwhelmed by all the information. Maybe she simply didn't understand.

The diagnostician completed her report and added, "We recommended a consultation with Dr. Goldsmith to further investigate the possibility of an attention deficit disorder."

The psychiatrist was a tall, spare man with graying hair and a face that Tonya would call weathered. What she liked best was his calm, matter-of-fact manner. "My examination confirmed an attention deficit disorder with hyperactivity," he said, and proceeded to explain the condition in laymen's terms, much as Karen had explained it to Tonya.

"People with ADHD," he said, "are chronic daydreamers."

Germain turned to Tonya and whispered, softly this time, "That's me."

Tonya glanced at Mrs. Parker. Did she get it?

Tonya knew *she* did. She'd been a daydreamer all her life. She guessed she'd spent enough hours staring out the window to term her woolgathering "chronic."

"They don't stay with one topic or one task very long," Dr. Goldsmith continued. "They have so much energy, they even have trouble staying in one place. Germain, does that sound like you?"

The boy ducked his head. "Yeah," he muttered.

Me, too, Tonya thought. During her school days she'd always had trouble staying in her seat. In her working life, she'd flitted from one job to another like the proverbial grasshopper, and she had the résumé to prove it.

"They get distracted by noise, by movement, even by their own thoughts," the doctor said. "Someone walks by in the hall outside the classroom, and there goes the math assignment."

"Yeah." This time Germain smiled.

Tonya smiled, too. Dr. Goldsmith could be describing her instead of Germain. In fact—

"People with ADHD are impulsive. They blurt out things without thinking, do things without thinking."

Just as she'd done a few minutes earlier when she'd snarled at Germain's mother, Tonya thought. Just as she'd done *all her life.*

Her heart began to pound. Dr. Goldsmith *was* describing her. She had all the symptoms, all the behaviors—damn it, all the problems of ADHD—and had ever since she could remember.

Maybe she wasn't the family flake. *Maybe* she had a reason, a good one. She bit her lip to keep from shouting out, "Is this me? Am I ADHD, too?"

The voices around her faded while she tried to quiet the voices in her head—the fear, the excitement.

Only when Dr. Goldsmith suggested that Germain start medication on a trial basis did Tonya again focus on the discussion. Mrs. Parker suddenly woke up, too. "How much it gonna cost for this medicine?"

"I'm sure it will be covered by Medicaid," Karen said.

"Better be or he don't get none."

"If not, perhaps we can investigate other funding," Karen said.

Even though her hands shook from her inner turmoil, Tonya made a note to talk to the Brewster Foundation about setting up a fund to underwrite such treatment.

"I'll write a prescription for Germain," Dr. Goldsmith said. "All right?"

Mrs. Parker, who had returned to contemplating her nails, managed a "Yeah" around her gum.

The remainder of the meeting was spent setting up an educational plan to help Germain catch up academically and develop self-management skills.

As soon as they adjourned, Tonya caught up with Dr. Goldsmith in the hall. She swallowed the lump in her throat. Over the din of students changing classes, she said, "May I ask you a question?"

"Certainly."

It was the most important question she'd ever asked. Heart slamming against her ribs, she said, "Can an adult have ADHD?"

"Yes, indeed."

The noise level in the hall increased. A tall boy in a baseball cap nearly knocked her over as he barreled past. Tonya barely noticed. "Do...do you see adults in your practice?"

"I do."

"Then," she said, feeling as if she were diving off the high board, "I'd like to make an appointment. When I listened to you in the conference, I felt like my life suddenly made sense."

The doctor smiled. "I'd be happy to see you, Ms. Brewster. When adults with ADHD hear it described, it's often an 'aha' experience." He fished in his pocket and handed her a card. "Call my office."

"I'll do that." She waved as he strode out of the building, then glanced around her. Here she stood, in the hallway of a grungy school in inner-city Houston, and maybe, just maybe, she'd found answers to questions she'd always had. Until now, she hadn't known where to find the answers. Fate, in the person of her grandfather, had sent her where she needed to go. Amazing.

She should call her granddad and tell him her suspicions about having ADHD, but first she'd talk to Kirk. She could hardly wait to tell him what she'd learned today. She'd shared a little of her lifelong frustration with him, but she hadn't told him everything. Now she wanted to confide the rest.

But first—

Thanking the Lord that someone had seen fit to invent

the cellular phone, she extracted hers from under the seat of the pickup and punched in the number of Dr. Goldsmith's office. This call couldn't wait.

"He can see you next Monday at ten," the receptionist told her.

Hallelujah! Tonya didn't even bother to write down the time. This was one appointment she wouldn't forget.

And now, she thought as she pulled into the lot at the center, to find Kirk.

Luckily, she saw him immediately, talking to Ladonna outside the building. In fact, *everyone* was outside the building. Why?

Then she noticed the police car parked in front. She jumped out of the truck and ran to Kirk, calling his name.

He turned toward her, his face like a thundercloud. If his eyes could shoot lightning bolts, she'd be dead right now.

"Wha—" she began, then her voice trailed off as he took a step toward her.

"We've been looking all over for you," he growled. "Where in hell have you been?"

This was what he was angry about? That she'd gone out without informing him? The heck with that! "I went to a meeting. I didn't know I needed your permission," she snapped, and tried to step past him. She'd ask Ramon what was going on.

She should have known better. Kirk's hand shot out and closed around her arm.

Swearing she wouldn't let him bully her, Tonya stood still in his grasp. "What is this," she demanded, "a police state?"

"Coming damn close," he muttered. "Rick found out the idea for Janene leaving town came from here, and he's mad as hell. We had a call thirty minutes ago. The Sabers are threatening to blow up the place."

14

TONYA SWALLOWED. "Oh," she managed to say. "The police—"

"The bomb squad's inside now."

"Have they...have they found the bomb?"

Kirk let out a tired sigh. "They haven't found anything." He pulled her around the corner of the building to a quiet spot. "When Rick surfaced again, I told the staff that no one was to go out alone. Did you forget?"

Tonya jerked her arm from his grasp. "No, but—"

"But what?" Kirk glared at her, arms folded across his chest. "Do you think because you're from the Brewster Foundation that you're above it all? That you don't have to abide by the rules here?"

"I—"

"Lady, you may hold the purse strings, but I'm in charge here and when you're on *my* turf, you do what I say." His voice, his stance, everything about him radiated anger.

He was mad? He hadn't seen "mad."

Tonya jabbed her finger into his chest. "Now, you listen to me. Number one—I went to Germain's school for a meeting that's been on the schedule for almost a month. All you had to do was look at the appointment book in Ramon's office. Number two—when I left, I knew nothing about another threat. It's been calm around here lately. *Everyone's* been going out alone. I'm no different from the rest of your staff."

"You are different."

"How?" She planted her hands on her hips and waited for his answer.

"The staff come from this neighborhood. They know their way around, know who to watch out for. You don't—"

"Belong here," she finished for him. She waited for him to deny it, but he stayed silent. That hurt. Badly. Tears stung her eyes. "I thought we'd gotten past that," she said tiredly. "I thought I'd proved myself. I guess not." She turned and walked away.

Kirk watched her go. Damn it, he'd almost had a heart attack when they hadn't been able to find her. He'd had all kinds of visions of what might have happened to her, everything from being held hostage by the Sabers to a thousand times worse.

And how had he handled it? Shot off his mouth the minute he'd seen her. Done just what she'd accused him of once before—acted like a damn Neanderthal.

He stuffed his hands in his pockets to hide the shaking and headed back to the front yard. There she was, in the midst of a group of pregnant girls, her arm around one of them. This was not the time to talk to her.

He'd try to explain to her later when they had some privacy. He wondered if she'd understand that he'd been more frightened than angry. He'd probably have to yell at her to convince her. The woman roused his temper almost as much as she stirred his passion.

The police officer who was in charge of the bomb squad appeared in the doorway and motioned to him. Kirk crossed the yard. "Found anything?"

"Nothing. Place is clean. You can send your folks back in now."

Kirk let out a breath of relief, then turned to relate the

news to the anxious group on the lawn. As they trooped in, he searched for Tonya, then saw her hurrying around the building toward the back entrance. Avoiding him. He could hardly blame her.

Before he had a chance to go after her, Ramon caught up with him and center business claimed him.

HALF AN HOUR LATER, Tonya was still upset. If she were a drinker, this would be the time for a drink. She wasn't, but she needed something to calm her down. Hot chocolate was her tranquilizer of choice, but it wasn't available here. She'd have to settle for tea.

She found Ladonna at the kitchen table, sipping coffee.

"Hi," Tonya said.

"Girlfriend, you don't look so good," Ladonna observed. "Kirk get to you?"

Tonya dumpèd a tea bag in hot water. "Yeah."

"You musta done the same to him. He doesn't look so good, either."

"Really?" Tonya stirred an extra spoonful of sugar into her tea. Anger always inspired a craving for sweets. "I'd expect him to be strutting around like a rooster. He put the outsider in her place."

Ladonna put a hand over Tonya's. "Girl, believe me. Whatever you two talked about, he's torn up about it. You know he's crazy about you."

"He picked an interesting way to show it. And, no, I don't know. He's...he's never said anything."

"Men," Ladonna snorted. "Their tongues are tangled up in knots. They never say what we need to hear."

"I'll drink to that." Tonya took a swallow of tea, burned her tongue and nearly dropped her cup.

"Kirk's all mixed up over you," Ladonna said, her lips

quirking. Then her smile faded. "He's got reasons for bein' in such a tizzy. He ever tell you about Amelia?"

"No. Who was she...or is she?"

"She *was* somebody who was important to him at one time. You ask him about her. Then maybe you'll understand him better." She stood and pushed in her chair. "I gotta get back to work." She started out of the kitchen, then paused. "You've been doin' a good job here. Don't let Mr. Butler be telling you different."

Tonya smiled after Ladonna. She appreciated getting a few strokes for what she'd done. But what had the other woman meant about Kirk's having his reasons for the way he'd acted earlier? And who was Amelia? An ex-wife? No, to her knowledge, Kirk had never been married. An ex-lover, she guessed. Did she really want to hear about the women in Kirk's life?

Yes.

She took her mug to the sink, washed it and headed for Kirk's door. It was open. She could see him hunched over his computer. He quit typing, ran a hand through his hair, then returned to the keyboard.

Without knocking, Tonya walked in and shut the door behind her. Kirk looked up and his expression turned wary. Good, she thought. His turn to feel the bite of nerves. "I want to talk to you," she said, and pulled a chair up to his desk. "I have some questions."

He nodded and turned off his computer. "I have things to say to you, too, but go ahead."

"Who was Amelia?"

His eyes registered shock, then suspicion. "How do you know about Amelia?"

"Ladonna mentioned her name. Oh, don't worry," she said, noting the quick flash of anger in his eyes. "She didn't tell me anything, just said I should ask."

"Amelia was...a girl I knew in college," Kirk said.

"Were you in love with her?"

He was silent for so long that Tonya almost decided he wasn't going to answer, but he finally said, "Yes."

"And?" she prompted.

"And it didn't work out."

"The end? That's all?" Impatiently, Tonya drummed her fingers on the edge of her chair. "Why don't you tell me the whole story?"

He let out a ragged sigh. "All right, but I don't see what it has to do with anything."

"Neither do I...yet. But go ahead."

"I told you part of it—that I got a football scholarship to the University of Texas. I was good. By my sophomore year I was a starter. By my junior year there was talk of a Heisman." He stared at the wall, gazing backward into the past. "You can't grow up in Texas without knowing how important football is at UT. My background didn't matter. Being a football player canceled that out and gave me an entry into the campus social whirl. I was a running back. On Saturdays I ran with the ball. The rest of the week girls ran after me. Who said, 'Power is a great aphrodisiac'? Well, so's football." He laughed suddenly. "It was great."

"I bet," Tonya said.

"I met Amelia in English class, spring semester of my junior year," he continued. "She was this dainty little blonde who belonged to the top sorority on campus. Her father ran an oil company out in Odessa. And here I was, a kid from the inner city with no fraternity pin, but she latched on to me."

Why not? Tonya thought. Any girl with eyes would pick Kirk out of a crowd.

"I never looked at another girl after that," he said. "Amelia and I dated all of our senior year. In April, just after I signed with the Eagles, we got engaged. We planned to get married after football season."

"What happened?"

"My injury happened," he said, as if that were self-explanatory.

"And?"

"And when she realized that my pro career was over, Amelia returned my ring. Since I didn't come from a rich family, she'd at least counted on the money that came from my football contract. And the celebrity that went with it. Very politely, she told me she wasn't interested in a has-been football player—she wanted the real thing." He let out a breath. "She started dating one of my teammates."

"What a bitch," Tonya said.

"Yeah, well..."

They sat silently for a few minutes. Tonya pondered what he had told her. Yes, he'd had an unhappy love affair, but what did that have to do with her and with her position at the OK Center?

The light dawned.

"You think because my family has money that I'm like Amelia, don't you? *Don't you?*" she insisted when he didn't answer. "It's all clear to me now," she said, swallowing angry tears. "You gave me all those little hints, but I missed them before. Your question about whether I was slumming the first time I came to your apartment. Your comments about Max, about my family. You think I'm an Amelia clone."

She jumped up from her chair and leaned over the desk, slapping her hands on it. "Well, I'm not. I never could be. I would never walk out on the man I loved because of an injury or any other kind of setback. If that's your picture of me, you don't know me at all."

Kirk looked miserable. "Tonya, I—"

She didn't bother letting him finish. She was revved up now. "And what about all those remarks about my not fitting in here? Was that about Amelia, too?"

"No, maybe the other was, but that part about not fitting in here was something else. You came here straight out of another world. You have no background in working with inner-city children."

"You're right," she said, "and I admit I've made mistakes. But I've learned, and I've accomplished something for the center. Know what happened this afternoon at Germain's school? No, of course you don't. You didn't give me a chance to tell you before. Well, I'll tell you now."

Because her emotional state threatened to make her legs give out, she sat down again and took a breath. Outside the door she could hear feet shuffling in the halls, muffled conversations. The after-school influx of kids had begun. She lowered her voice.

"Germain has an attention deficit disorder. They're going to work with him, help him. Maybe he'll be a success story instead of a kid with an attitude. I got that going. *Me.* All you saw was that I overstepped my authority when I offered to let him work around here. All you see is my mistakes." She took a breath and went on. "All you do is berate me. Just because I went out this afternoon—"

"I apologize for that," he said. "I wasn't angry."

"You could have fooled me."

"Damn it, Tonya, I was scared out of my mind that something had happened to you."

"You saw that nothing did."

"And I still yelled," he admitted. "I'm sorry. And you know, you're wrong that I just see your mistakes," he said wearily. "I told your grandfather how much you've contributed here."

"But did you mean it?"

"Of course," he said.

Tonya sighed. "I hear a 'but' coming."

Kirk spread his hands. "Tonya, for me, this is my life's work. For you, it's a short-term diversion."

Fury leapt up and almost clogged her throat. "You don't know that."

"Didn't you tell me you have a short attention span?"

"Yes, I did. I realized today I have an attention deficit like Germain. But what I've done at the center, what I've found here.... I don't know. It's different." She tried to find the words she needed to explain her feelings, but they eluded her. "Oh, what's the use?" she said, rising. "No matter what I say, you won't believe me. You won't trust me. You may not believe I'm Amelia, but you'll always see me as a misfit here. I wasn't born in the right neighborhood. Well, I can't change that." She glanced at her watch. "It's getting late. I'm going home." At the door she hesitated with her hand on the knob for a moment. When he said nothing, she pulled the door open. "Goodbye, Kirk."

Slowly, she trudged down the hall. What hurt most was that he didn't come after her.

ON MONDAY TONYA SAT in Dr. Goldsmith's office. She wasn't in the best of spirits. The weekend had crawled by with no word from Kirk. Fine, she'd decided. If that was the way he wanted it, that's what he'd get.

This morning she'd called Ramon to tell him she had a doctor's appointment and wouldn't be in today. She wasn't sure she'd be in tomorrow, either. She wasn't sure she'd be in *ever*.

Now, as she awaited the doctor's diagnosis, she felt strangely numb. Kirk's distrust had hurt her badly. She wondered if severe pain dulled your nerve endings.

Or perhaps she was overstressed. She'd worried all

weekend about the bomb threat, fearing the Sabers would break in while the building was vacant. Again, nothing had happened. Maybe they were just trying to scare everyone to death.

"Ms. Brewster." Dr. Goldsmith came in and sat behind his desk. "I've looked at your test results and at the questionnaire you filled out. My preliminary diagnosis is ADD. As you know, that stands for attention deficit disorder. We'll want to do some further testing to confirm the diagnosis, but I'm reasonably sure we will." He looked at her intently. "How does that make you feel?"

She considered, then gave him a wry smile. "I guess like I've had good news and bad news. The good news is there's a name for what's been bugging me all my life. The bad news is it won't go away."

"Succinctly put," the doctor said. "But we can temper the bad news. As I mentioned during Germain's conference, we can minimize the effects of ADD."

"How?"

"Well, from what you told me, you're already doing a pretty good job yourself. You keep a calendar, write things down. We can help you even more with self-management skills."

"Like you're going to do with Germain."

He nodded. "That's a big part of ADD treatment. Another is finding the right niche. A job where the ADD adult can make use of her strengths and talents. And just as important, a job that doesn't tap into your weaknesses. From what you've told me about your present position, you've found that niche."

Tonya thought of Kirk. Could she go back and face him every day? Work in the same building? Passing him in the hall would have her reeling with pain. Besides…. "I…I don't know," she said. "My grandfather sent me there as a representative of the family foundation on a short-term basis."

"You may want to rethink that, find a way to make the position permanent."

Sadly, she shook her head. "I may not be able to...for personal reasons."

"I see."

He didn't probe and Tonya didn't volunteer anything further. The pain was too new, too sharp to deal with, even in a psychiatrist's office.

"We have a support group for adults with attention deficit. You may find that helpful. And I'm also going to give you the names of some books on adult ADD." He wrote some information down on a prescription pad.

"Will I need to take medication, like Germain?"

"You may, but we'll decide that later. Any other questions?"

"Not now. I'm sure I'll think of dozens."

"If you do, call. On your way out, talk to Eleanor about scheduling the rest of those tests." He rose, they shook hands, and Tonya left his office.

So now she had a name for her skittishness and for the problems that had always plagued her. She was relieved. She *should* be relieved to have learned that she wasn't the family black sheep because she was just a flake. She actually had a reason.

So why wasn't she ecstatic?

That was easy to answer. And it had nothing to do with the diagnosis. It was because of Kirk Butler. He hadn't cared enough to call to talk things over. And darned if she'd call him. No way would she go crawling back to him. She had her pride.

"WHAT DO YOU MEAN she's not here?" Kirk growled at Ladonna. "Where the hell is she?"

"I don't know. All I heard is what Ramon said. She didn't come in this morning." She cocked her head. "You have anything to do with that?"

He didn't answer. Instead, he stalked out of her office and back to his own. Once there, he glared at the telephone. It stared mutely back at him, just as his home phone had all weekend. Damn, he should have known better than to expect to hear from Tonya.

Okay, he hadn't been totally fair with her. He'd equated her with Amelia, and maybe he was wrong. On the other hand, he'd trusted Amelia, too, and look where that had gotten him. On the third hand—

With a snarl of frustration, he went down the hall and pounded on Ramon's door. Before Ramon could respond, Kirk shoved the door open and strode in.

"Get up on the wrong side of the bed, *amigo?*" Ramon asked mildly.

Kirk ignored the question. "Why didn't Tonya come in this morning?"

"She said she had a doctor's appointment."

Kirk was alarmed now rather than angry. "Is she sick?"

"Didn't say."

Maybe he should call. Back in his office, he tried her apartment but got no answer. Not only that, but she'd turned off her answering machine. He continued calling for the rest of the morning and all afternoon without success. How long could a doctor's appointment take? Was she in the hospital?

Knowing Tonya, she'd had a routine doctor's appointment and gotten distracted on her way home, probably stopped off at a mall. Yes, he reassured himself, she was undoubtedly on a shopping spree.

Still, he drove by her apartment that evening. No one answered the door. He drove to the back and checked her garage. It was empty. He hung around for a while, but she didn't show up. All right, he decided, he'd talk to her in the morning. He went home and spent a restless night.

The next day he arrived at the center early. Tonya didn't come in.

"She called and said she would be out of town the next few days," Ramon said in answer to Kirk's question. "When she gets back, she'll let us know her plans."

"Her...plans? What the hell does that mean?"

Ramon shrugged. "Beats me. Maybe we already measured up to her grandfather's criteria and the foundation will continue to fund us, so she won't have to come back."

Not come back? Kirk didn't want to think of that. But then, why should she? He'd done everything in his power to drive her away. "Yeah, just like we predicted in the beginning," he said in a feeble attempt to make light of the situation. "Back to the country club. She's had enough."

"I don't know," Ramon said, frowning. "I got the impression she liked it here."

"Maybe not enough," Kirk said.

Back in his office, he scowled at the wall. She'd done what he wanted, gotten out of his way. But couldn't she at least have called and told him she wouldn't be back?

She could bet her life he wouldn't call her, he thought. No matter how much he missed her. After all, he had his pride.

15

"I'M SORRY, GRANDDAD. I'd rather not go back." Clint had been out of town for a few days and this was her first chance to meet with him. Now, seated on the pale damask sofa in her grandparents' living room, Tonya curled her feet under her and hugged a pillow.

"What's this?" Clint Brewster's heavy brows furrowed in disapproval. "Are you giving up on another job?"

"I'm not giving up," Tonya protested. "The center is running fine. I wrote a report for the foundation. See?" She reached into the purse she'd dropped on the floor, dug out a set of papers and handed them to Clint.

He scanned the report, nodding, then looked up. "Looks good, but we stipulated six months' trial. The six months is nowhere near over. You'd have to bring this before the foundation board, ask for a vote."

"I know we need an emergency board meeting, but I have a reason. Lots of reasons." She proceeded to enumerate them all. The staff didn't want her there in the first place. She'd put her foot in her mouth on too many occasions. The place was dangerous. "We had a bomb threat the other day. Did you know that?"

Her grandfather shook his head, and she saw the flash of emotion in his eyes as he reached out to stroke her hair. "I don't recall you worrying about the hazards of Third World countries during your travels."

"No-o..."

"Well then." He spoke as if everything were settled. He

might fear the danger to her but he'd never settle for her running away.

She took a breath. "It's not that I don't like the work. I love it. I've finally found my niche." She smiled as she realized she'd repeated Dr. Goldsmith's term. "I may not go back to the OK Center, but lots of agencies do the same kind of work. I could find a job in one of those—a real job this time."

Her grandfather frowned. "If you like it so much, why not stay where you are?"

"I have another reason. One of the directors, Kirk Butler—" Horrified that she'd blurted out his name, she pressed her lips together.

"That the fellow you brought to my birthday party?" She nodded, and her grandfather said, "Seemed like a nice young man to me. I thought you two looked like you were sort of sweet on each other."

Tonya couldn't help smiling at the old-fashioned term, but the smile didn't last long. "I'm in love with him." She felt the tears that had continually lodged just behind her eyes these past few days, and blinked to stop them.

"Now, why should that make you sad?"

"He thinks I'm a rich bitch like his old girlfriend."

"Seems to me," her grandfather said, "that would make you mad, not sad. Mad enough to show him what a Brewster's made of. What *you're* made of."

"What am I made of, Granddad?" she muttered. "I've never been like the rest of the family."

He frowned again, this time looking puzzled. "What do you mean by that?"

"I'm the one who always tags along behind. The loser in a pack of winners."

"Tonya Jane Brewster." His voice was stern. "Who told you that?"

Tonya pulled a tissue from her purse and blew her nose. "Nobody had to spell it out for me. I just knew."

"That's the most ridiculous thing I ever heard." Disgust laced his voice. "I just read your report. The woman who talked these police officers into volunteering their time to work with inner-city kids, the woman who's organizing a fund-raiser, the woman who got this youngster tested? Young lady, you're a champion. You're made of the same stuff as every other Brewster."

Tonya stared at him in shock.

"Close your mouth, girl," Clint instructed. "Look at what you've accomplished. Why, if you'd stick with one job for a change, there's no telling how far you would go."

"That's just it, Granddad. I never stick with anything. I flit around from one thing to another. I...I just learned I have an attention deficit disorder."

"And what the hell is that?" Clint blustered.

She explained what she'd learned at the doctor's office yesterday.

Clint listened quietly, then asked, "You think now that you've found out about this, you're going to be a different person?"

"Maybe a more organized person, but I'm afraid I won't change the basic me."

"That's a relief," Clint said, leaning back in his chair. "For a minute there, I was afraid you'd say you were going to turn as stuffy as your cousin Claudia."

Tonya's mouth fell open. "You think Claudia's stuffy?"

"What do you take me for, young lady? Just because I've had another birthday, you think I've lost my wits? Of course Claudia's stuffy. Stuffy, stodgy and stiff as a board. Always has been, always will be."

Tonya burst out laughing. "Granddad, you devil."

"So," Clint said when her laughter had died down, "are

you going to let this attention disorder get the best of you? Or are you going to beat it?"

Tonya's chin rose automatically. "Beat it. Damn it, I'm going to beat it."

"That's a Brewster for you," Clint said, nodding in satisfaction. "Now, what about this Butler you've been shedding tears over? Is he worth it?"

"Definitely worth it."

"And you think he's the right man for you?" Clint asked.

"At first glance, we seem totally wrong for each other, but I know we're right."

"Well then, all you have to do is make him see it, too."

"Easier said than done," Tonya muttered.

Her grandfather cupped her chin with his big hand. "I didn't hear that and you didn't say it. My granddaughter would never let some fellow beat her down."

Tonya couldn't help smiling at that. "Maybe you're right," she said.

"Maybe?"

"For sure you're right." Clint nodded in satisfaction, and Tonya continued. "I have to go to El Paso tomorrow to arrange a mystery weekend for Betsy at Whodunit. But I'll be back."

Clint's eyes twinkled. "And when you come back, you'll go over to that Our Kids Center and give that fellow Kirk what for."

"I will. If I have to hog-tie him and drag him in, I'll make him see how right we are together."

Tonya suddenly felt her grandmother's hand on her shoulder. "Tonya, dear, are you talking about a man or a rodeo bronc?"

She laughed. "Same thing, Grandmother."

"SAM, THIS IS Kirk Butler."

"Yes?" Samantha Phillips's voice was chilly.

Kirk shifted uncomfortably on the hard chair in his office. "I'm trying to locate Tonya."

There was a long pause, then Sam said, "I believe she's meeting with Betsy Potter at the mystery bookstore this morning, then leaving town."

"Leaving? She's leaving?" His heartbeat shot up.

"Yes, for El Paso."

"But she's coming back." He didn't phrase it as a question. She *had* to come back.

Sam's voice cooled a few more degrees. "I assume so, but why don't you ask *her*?"

She knew damn well why. He could hear it in her voice. Aware how close they were, he knew that if he'd made Tonya angry, she'd have told Sam. "Tonya and I had a...misunderstanding."

"Mmm."

"If you talk to her before she leaves, tell her I'm trying to reach her."

"I don't think so," Sam said. "I think you should take care of that yourself."

"Damn it, I've been trying. She doesn't answer her phone. She's not at her town house." He took a breath to stifle his frustration. "I know she had a doctor's appointment on Monday. I don't even know why."

"I'm sure she'll explain, but I'll ease your mind. She isn't sick."

"Thanks." He was relieved to hear that, glad Sam had relented enough to tell him. He disconnected and tried Tonya's one more time. Still no answer. Then he tried the mystery bookstore, hoping someone would pick up even if business hours hadn't started yet. No one did. Damn, he'd drive over to Whodunit right now if the assistant police chief for this area wasn't coming over in fifteen minutes to meet with the center directors.

When she gets back, he promised himself. Then they'd talk

things over, work something out. A live-in arrangement until they decided if they were really right for each other. He could handle that.

They'd discuss the disorder she thought she had, too. He'd driven past a bookstore the other day and found a book on attention deficit disorders and begun reading. He wanted to understand what made her the person she was.

Satisfied that he'd solved his dilemma over Tonya, he got back to work. The meeting with the assistant police chief went as scheduled, and for the first time in several days Kirk felt as if he was back to normal. Amazing how coming to a decision could change things.

Then the fire alarm in the hall went off.

"Damn!" Kirk muttered. They'd had several fire drills since the Sabers' threat, and here was another. He glanced at the pile of papers on his desk. He was behind on just about everything, thanks to his mooning over Tonya for the past few days. He heard footsteps hurrying down the hall, but he was tempted to skip the fire drill and continue working.

Then he heard shouts.

He glanced down and saw a gray curl of smoke spiraling under his door. No drill. Good God, this was a real fire. The Sabers! he thought.

Cautiously, he felt the doorknob. It wasn't hot, so he opened the door slowly. Down the hall, smoke billowed from an open doorway.

The day-care center.

As he ran toward the room, smoke filled his nostrils. He began to cough. "Anyone in there?" he shouted.

No answer. But smoke could have overcome them—

He heard sounds behind him and turned. A teenage girl ran toward him with Corelle at her heels.

"Shawnetta, stop!" Corelle yelled, but the girl kept on.

"My baby. She's in there." Eyes wild, hands outstretched, Shawnetta tried to dodge past Kirk.

He caught her, held her still. "You can't go in."

The girl kicked him. "Let me go. I have to get her." She bit his hand, drew blood.

"Help me keep her still," he shouted to Corelle. The hallway was filling with smoke. They didn't have much time. "Where's your baby?"

"I told you. In there."

"You have to tell me *where*." Shawnetta didn't answer. Her eyes had gone blank. Kirk shook her. "Damn it. Tell me where she is."

"Playpen," she sobbed. "Back corner."

"Get Shawnetta out," Kirk yelled to Corelle. He pulled off his shirt, soaked it at the water fountain near the daycare room and held it over his face.

Crouching, he edged into the room. Now he could hear the crackle of flames, see them devouring the beanbag chair where Janene had sat a few weeks ago. Rick did this, he thought as he dropped to his knees. His eyes smarted, his lungs filled with smoke. Soon the oxygen would be gone. Could the baby have survived this long?

But he heard a weak cry. He had to go on.

Feeling his way, he inched toward the corner. Hot. It was so hot. *Got to...keep...going. Got to...get her out.* And he had to get himself out, too. If he didn't, he'd never see Tonya again. Never have a chance to tell her he loved her.

A shape loomed in front of him. The playpen. He could barely make out the tiny figure slumped in one corner.

No breath left, he thought, but he had to reach the infant. What if it were his baby? His and Tonya's?

He reached out and touched the playpen. Hot! He could feel blisters pop out on his hand. Ignoring the pain, he rose, reached inside and grabbed the baby. Its hands flailed weakly as he lifted it.

Now, out. He wrapped his shirt around the infant and crawled back toward the door, cradling the child in one arm as he'd once cradled a football. He moved fast this time. Hot ash fell on his back. Flames licked at his shoes, smoke obscured his vision...

Can't go any farther. His movements slowed. He thought of Tonya. *Too late... So damned sorry...*

TONYA PULLED ONTO the freeway, heading toward Intercontinental Airport. She drove her Jaguar today, and the dashboard clock read twelve o'clock. As usual, she'd gotten a late start. Would she have time to park and make her El Paso flight?

She switched on the radio and searched for music. Instead she got news.

"In local news, a two-alarm blaze is raging at an innercity facility. Arson is suspected in the fire at the Our Kids Center on Magnolia Street on Houston's east side."

"Our Kids. Oh, my God."

Where was the next exit? She had to get off this blasted freeway and turn around. "Tell me what's happening," she muttered at the radio news commentator as she swerved around a van and into the lane for the off ramp.

"A male staff member has been reported missing—"

"Kirk!" Every ounce of blood seemed to drain from her body.

"Possibly inside the building."

No, not Kirk. Not anyone. Let it be a mistake. She shot down the ramp. A prayer on her lips, she careened around a corner and headed back, dodging other cars, speeding through yellow lights, even a couple of red ones. Damn, where was a cop when you needed one? She could use a police escort.

The newscaster shifted to an item about a proposed tax hike by the county. Tonya fiddled with the radio dial as she drove. Nothing more about the fire. She turned back to the station she'd first heard the news on, hoping for further information. Nothing.

Then, a few minutes later: "That fire at the Our Kids Center is still raging. Sources say the center received a threatening call several days ago from someone who identified himself as a member of a juvenile gang. Police are looking for the alleged gang member."

"Rick," Tonya muttered. If the courts didn't lock him up for good this time, they were crazy.

"No word on the missing staff member, who is thought to have gone into the building to search for an infant still in the day-care center," the commentator continued.

Doesn't mean they haven't found him, Tonya tried to reassure herself. *It just means the newscaster doesn't have the information yet.* She knew it was Kirk. He'd be the one brave enough—or foolhardy enough—to rush in to rescue a baby. *Don't let him die. I need him. I love him.*

Magnolia Street materialized before her. As she made the turn, she vowed she wouldn't break down no matter how bad the news was that awaited her, then prayed she wouldn't have to keep that promise.

As she came within sight of the OK Center, she saw cars parked on either side of the street, a fire engine, two police cars and an ambulance. She'd have to park here and go the rest of the way on foot.

She got out of the car, slammed the door and ran. People thronged the yard at the center, all of them milling about, pointing, chattering. Heart pounding, Tonya raced down the sidewalk. The smell of smoke and charred wood met her nostrils.

She looked anxiously for someone who could tell her what was going on. Ladonna stood alone, staring at the building. Tonya rushed to her side. "Where's Kirk?"

Ladonna didn't question Tonya's sudden appearance. "Inside," she said, and Tonya saw that she was crying.

She didn't stay to comfort Ladonna. Instead, she ran toward the building. She had to find someone—anyone—who could tell her about Kirk. She shoved through the crowd, elbowing people aside, moving blindly forward—

"Hey!" A hand gripped her arm, held her in place.

She barely spared the young firefighter a glance. "Let me go." She jerked her arm.

"You can't go in there."

She knew that, but— "I have to—"

"Lady." He dragged her back a step. "Can't you see there's a fire? You can't go any closer."

"I know." Tears streamed down her face. "But there's a man inside. I have to find him."

The sandy-haired young man glanced around as if looking for help. "They've gone in after him. They'll get him out. Come on now," he coaxed, "you sit down over there, and as soon as they find him, I'll let you know, okay?" His voice was quiet now, but he didn't let go of her arm.

"Please." She tried to pull away.

Agitated now, he took her shoulders and forcibly sat her on the ground. "Lady, do us both a favor and sit down so I can get back to work, or...or, damn it, I'll have you arrested."

Tonya gave him one defiant glare, but she didn't get up when he dashed off. Eyes on the doorway of the building, she prayed.

"HERE HE IS!"

Voices, footsteps. Kirk saw black boots. Firefighters. One of them reached for the baby, someone else gripped Kirk under his arms and dragged him into the hall. A mask was shoved over his face. He coughed once, twice, then drew in a breath.

"Let's get them out of here."

Arms grasped him, but he pushed them away. "No," he managed to say, and struggled to his feet. He'd walk out under his own power. When he got outside, he'd sit for a while until he could breathe again. Then, by God, he was getting on the next plane for El Paso. Wherever Tonya was, he'd find her and bring her home.

God, he was dizzy. He staggered, and the firefighter caught his arm. "Door's right in front of us, sir. You'd better let the medics have a look at you. Here we are." He opened the door, and Kirk stumbled outside.

Someone—a paramedic, he guessed—led him away from the building. "I'm okay," he insisted. "The baby?"

"We're going to take a look at it. Sit down. I'll be right back."

The fellow didn't have to ask him twice. He slid down and leaned against a tree, marveling at how many people were milling around. Even a TV cameraperson.

He shut his eyes and Tonya's face swam into view. He'd have a chance to tell her how he felt after all. And he'd do it.

He'd had enough of this playing around. He was in love with her. All the way in love.

So they had some differences. They'd work them out. If the woman thought she was going to walk out of here, go back to her world and forget about him, she'd better think again. He'd lay it on the line, tell her he loved her, ask her to be his wife.

Oh, God, he thought, opening his eyes and fighting to subdue the butterflies dancing in his stomach, he was actually thinking about getting married. Maybe it was the smoke inhalation.

No, it was real.

Hell, if a tough guy like Wade Phillips could survive it,

so could he. Never let it be said that Kirk Butler took second place to any man when it came to toughness.

He smiled and closed his eyes again.

FROM AROUND THE CORNER of the building, Tonya saw the young firefighter coming toward her, waving his arm. "We got him out, lady," he called. "He's okay."

She leapt up and ran.

She came up behind him. He sat beneath a tree, a paramedic squatting in front of him. He was shirtless, covered with soot. But alive. Safe. She saw bandages on his back; his hair was singed. Oh, God, he looked wonderful.

Tonya dropped to her knees beside him. "Kirk!"

At her words, he turned. "Tonya." His voice was hoarse.

He started to get up, but the paramedic put a hand on his arm. "Just one minute, sir. We're almost done."

Kirk barely glanced at the man wrapping gauze around his hand. His eyes were on Tonya.

Tonya heard someone come up behind her, but she kept her gaze fixed on Kirk. They were close but not close enough. She wanted to touch him, gather him into her arms. Dear heaven, she'd come so close to losing him.

He looked at her as if the crowd milling around them didn't matter, as if they were the only two people here, as if—

"All finished, sir. It wouldn't hurt for you to go to the hospital and get checked out."

Kirk rose. Tonya got to her feet. In an instant, they were in each other's arms, holding tight, kissing hard.

Tonya drew away. "Kirk, I was so worried, so scared. Are you really all right?"

"Sure."

She lifted his palm. Along the edges of the gauze wrapped around his hand, she saw reddened skin. "You went back in."

He shook his head. "I was already in. One of the babies was left in the nursery. If I'd waited for the fire department to get here, even as fast as they are, she'd have died."

"You could have died, too," she whispered, touching his cheek.

"Yes, but I didn't, and I'm fine."

She buried her face against his chest and burst into tears.

"Hey," he said, cupping her chin and tilting her face up, "I told you I was okay. What's wrong?"

She sniffled. "I promised myself I wouldn't cry, no matter what, and look at me."

She put her arms around his waist and held him close. Being with him again felt so good. So right.

He drew away and cupped her cheek with one hand. "What are you doing here? Sam said you'd gone to El Paso."

"I was on my way to the airport when I heard about the fire on the news. They said a staff member was inside."

"And you came back," he said wonderingly, as if he couldn't believe it was true.

"Of course I did," she said, amazed that he would doubt it. "This place is part of my life. And I knew the staff member in the building had to be you. I figured if I had to go in and drag you out myself, I would. No way would I lose the man I love."

He stared at her. "Say that again," he whispered.

"I said, No way would I lose the man I love." She stepped back and put her hands on her hips. "I love you, Kirk. You'll just have to learn to live with it."

"That shouldn't be a hardship. I love you, too."

"Well," she said, and tossed her head, "for a street-smart guy, you certainly took long enough to realize it."

He chuckled and hugged her close again. "I can't believe I wasted so much time. Love was staring me in the face all along." He bent his head and placed a tender kiss on her lips. "How about spending the rest of our lives learning to live with it? Is that long enough?"

Tonya's eyes widened. "Are we talking marriage?"

"We sure are."

"In that case, yes." She stood on tiptoe and kissed him again, hard. The sound of applause had them springing apart. Ladonna, Ramon and several of the staff stood a few feet away, unabashedly watching and listening. Even the sandy-haired fireman was among the group. "Mister, you better believe this lady would have gotten you out. I almost had to call a cop to keep her outa there."

"Hey, it's nice to have some good news along with the bad. Congratulations," Ladonna said. The others added their good wishes, too.

"Kirk, I've talked to the fire marshal," Ramon said. "We have to keep out of the building until they finish their inspection. Probably be tomorrow before we can go inside. Why don't you two take off? I'm sure you have a lot to talk about."

"I can't just walk away."

"Sure you can," Ramon said. "Everything's under control here. Besides, the paramedic told you to get some rest. If we need you, we'll call."

"Well then," Tonya agreed, "you have to go. You can take care of the center later. Now we're going to take care of you."

As she tugged at his arm, Kirk muttered, "Are you going to be a bossy wife?"

"You bet I am. Come on. I'm parked right down the street."

They were halfway across the yard when Ramon hailed them.

"Now what?" Tonya muttered.

Ramon dashed up. "We just got word they picked up Rick and two of his buddies. I'm going down to the station.

This time we're going to see that he's put away for a long time."

"Damn right." Kirk hesitated. "I should come with you."

"No way," Tonya said. "You're coming with *me*." She led him down the street to her car.

All four wheels were gone.

"I told you before, if you parked this vehicle on the street, you were asking for trouble," Kirk said sternly.

"And where else was I going to park it?" She raised her purse over her head.

This time Kirk was prepared. He caught the bag with his good hand and wrenched it away before it came down on him. Laughing, he pulled Tonya close. "We're going to have a hell of an interesting life."

Tonya kissed his cheek. "We certainly are."

TWO WEEKS LATER the announcement of the engagement of Tonya Jane Brewster and Kirk Allan Butler, both staff members at the Our Kids Center, appeared in the Houston *Express*. The article mentioned that in honor of their engagement, the Brewster Foundation had given an additional grant to the center so that when repairs were made after a recent fire, the building could be enlarged. The addition would make the center the largest of its kind in the state.

It's hot...and it's out of control!

**This spring, Temptation turns up the heat.
Look for these bold, provocative,
*ultra*sexy books!**

Available in April 1997:

OUTRAGEOUS by Lori Foster

He was totally outrageous! One minute, the sexy-as-sin
cop was rescuing Emily Cooper from drunken hoodlums.
Five minutes later, he was tearing his clothes off in front of
a group of voracious women. What kind of man was he...
and why couldn't Emily keep her hands off him? Little did
she know that Judd Sanders really *was* a cop, whose
"cover" left him a little too *uncovered* for his liking.

BLAZE—Red-hot reads—from

You are cordially invited to a

HOMETOWN REUNION

September 1996—August 1997

Bad boys, cowboys, babies. Feuding families,
arson, mistaken identity, a mom on the run...
Where can you find romance and adventure?
Tyler, Wisconsin, that's where!

So join us in this not-so-sleepy little town and
experience the love, the laughter and the
tears of those who call it home.

WELCOME TO A
HOMETOWN REUNION

Daphne Sullivan and her little girl were hiding
from something or someone—that much was
becoming obvious to those who knew her. But
from whom? Was it the stranger with the dark
eyes who'd just come to town? Don't miss
Muriel Jensen's *Undercover Mom,* ninth in a
series you won't want to end....

Available in May 1997
at your favorite retail store.

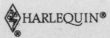

HARLEQUIN®

Look us up on-line at: http://www.romance.net   HTR9

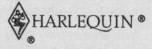

LOVE *or* MONEY?
Why not Love *and* Money!
After all, millionaires
need love, too!

How to Marry a MILLIONAIRE

Suzanne Forster,
Muriel Jensen
and
Judith Arnold

bring you three original stories
about finding that one-in-a million man!

Harlequin also brings you
a million-dollar sweepstakes—enter
for your chance to win a fortune!

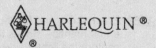 HARLEQUIN ®
®

HTMM

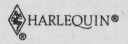
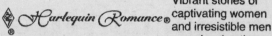

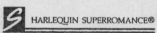